PURSUIT

PURSUIT

NEW ORLEANS ROGUES: BOUDREAUX
BOOK 1

QUINN MARLOWE

sp

PB ISBN: 979-8-9988311-2-6
LOC information available upon request
cover by Mayflower designs

HEADS UP!

If you've ready any of my books, you know I tend to tread on the lighter side of dark. My characters like to be spicy and funny, and I've never felt I needed to include any warnings.

This book is different. In the following pages you'll find murder, child abuse (off page), non-con touching (on page), torture (on page), human trafficking (on page), and general skullduggery. This book might not be for everyone, so please consider your own needs before reading.

NOTE FROM THE AUTHOR

This one hit hard.

It also turned out a whole lot bigger than I expected it to be. Not that I should be surprised by that. Brooks is always catching me off-guard.

Quick dedication, here. This one is for the girls and guys who want to be able to do everything themselves and take on the whole world... but who also want someone to come save them when they have a plan that goes wrong.

And who inevitably hate that they want that.

Fam, let yourself want a hero in your life. Because we all deserve a Lucien Boudreaux looking out for us. Even if we're doing our best to be Brooks Peterson.

#LessonsLearnedFromTwoYearsofTherapy

Love you all. Hope you have as much fun on this Brooks-planned adventure as I did. It has just as many bad ideas, and just as much spice, as you'd expect from our girl.

xoxo,

-Q

1

BROOKS

This isn't how anything was supposed to go.

To start with, I'm not supposed to be in this apartment.

In this crumbling row house.

In fucking Brooklyn.

Christ.

I shove my way through the kitchen, kicking at the stain on the floor as I go, and pull up next to the coffee maker. That's not up to snuff, either. If I'm guessing, I'd say it's at least ten years old, and looks like someone was using it in some sort of scientific experiment.

One that included acid.

I snort at the thought and put it in my back pocket, because I've never worked with acid before. It sounds... interesting. That brings an even bigger smile to my face, and for a moment I actually feel better.

Then I look outside at the cold, dreary sky and fall serious again.

I reach for the cupboard and grab a mug–dirty, just like the rest of this place–and pour a cup of coffee. I don't like the fact that there's no cream or chocolate for it, but it is what it is.

Beggars can't exactly be choosers, right?

I step through the door and out onto what passes for a porch, and slide into the one chair out here. The weather is cold and rainy, and any sane person would stay inside, but I've been here for three days and I'm sick of the tiny apartment. The beige walls. The dirty carpet. I miss my big bed and fluffy towels and the enormous sound system I had installed when I moved into my place.

I miss the security of knowing I'm in one of the safest buildings in all of New York.

I want to go home.

I take a sip of coffee and pull the butterfly knife out of my back pocket, where I've been storing it. A quick flip of my wrist and the thing opens, the blade whirring to life like it's greeting me.

"Hello, old friend," I murmur.

Another flip and it's closed, but the moment the shine of the steel disappears I realize I'm not ready to say goodbye to it yet. So I keep flipping. Open, closed. Open, closed. Sharp, dull. Exposed, hidden.

Protected, and not protected.

Feels a lot like my life lately.

I put the knife away and shake myself, then take another deep sip of the coffee. I need the caffeine to start working its magic, because I'm not here to mope around and cry to myself. The fact that I'm sitting here making up metaphors about a freaking knife is stupid and pointless.

A metaphor for what's going on in my head, if you will.

"Right," I breathe.

Well, that's enough of that.

I step to the railing that surrounds the small balcony and look to the sky, marshaling my thoughts and every sneaky instinct in my body. I didn't come here for the view, and I sure as hell didn't do it for my health.

Hell, I'm probably destroying my lungs by exposing them to whatever mold is growing in this building.

But I didn't have a choice, because my apartment might be in one of the most expensive buildings in New York, but it's also not safe. Too many people know my address. They came for us already, once, and arrived again directly after the battle, barging into my apartment like they had a fucking right to be there and trying to take me with them.

Worst of all, I'm not even positive who 'they' are.

Because we defeated one set of them, in the war on the streets of New York last week–the war where we finished Sylvester Poffo and his enormous crew of Italian mafia. We also took out some of the Massimos, and all of the Carusos. And that should have been all there was to it. The Rossis and Brennans should have been safe, and I should have been able to go back to my normal life.

Unfortunately, that's not how it's turned out. Someone is still after me, which means we have enemies I don't know about.

Which is a problem.

I turn my eyes away from the grayed-out sky and look to the road below me, eyes narrowed at the thought, and jerk to a stop at what I see down there.

A row of dark vans file along so slowly they're holding up the traffic behind them. Blacked-out windows. No doors. Totally anonymous, except for the fact that they look like they're in some sort of funeral procession.

Trying so hard to blend into the background that they stand out like a man with a gun pointed at your head.

And just like that I'm flying back through time, my world spinning around me like I'm caught in Dorothy's tornado and events making almost as much sense. A blink and I'm back in

New Orleans again, the gray sky of New York changing out for a pitch-black night sky full of stars and moisture, the air thick with the scent of mildew and magnolias around me.

Summertime in Louisiana.

And a house so big I used to get lost in the corridors before I figured out how to run them without losing my way.

I'm only thirteen, and I'm staring out the window of my bedroom with my lip caught between my teeth and the air stuck in my lungs, unable to breathe. Barely able to think. Definitely not able to scream.

Outside, in the driveway of my father's house, a row of vans is pulling up the drive, their black edges melting into the midnight air around them as they make their way up the cobblestones. They're as quiet as death, and nearly as creepy.

And I would think that they're a figment of my imagination. Vans that don't actually exist, floating up the driveway beneath the moss-hung trees of the yard, their tires making almost no noise and their engines already cut. It would be easy to think I'm just dreaming, or that I'm seeing things. Visions left over from one of the books I've been reading, or from a show I watched on TV.

Except I've seen these sorts of vans before, and I know what's in them.

I watch until they park in front of the house, then cringe when men start getting out of them. They're all in black, and though they're not the men I see in the house during the day, I recognize them.

Because I've seen them before, too.

When one of them suddenly looks up at the house, I duck back behind the curtain, a scream trapped in my throat and a prayer on my lips. I'm not supposed to be up at this time of night, and I'm sure as hell not supposed to be looking out my window at what's going on downstairs. I don't have to ask anyone to know that much. Nothing good happens in this house during the day.

Worse things happen at night.

I peek around the curtain with one eye, looking for the man who was staring at the house, but he's already moved on. He's pulling the back doors of one of the vans open, now, and gesturing violently to whoever is back there. Other men are doing the same behind the other vans, their gestures just as violent, though none of them is saying anything.

The air outside is still heavy with silence and the deep secrets of the night.

Within moments, the girls start getting out of the vans. They're just as quiet, though I can see from the shaking of their shoulders that they're sobbing. Their hands are shaking, their faces turned to the ground as if they don't want to see what's going to happen to them. I don't have to see their expressions to know that they've been beaten into submission and told that terrible things will happen if they dare to make a sound.

I recognize the turn of their shoulders. The tension that tells me they've already had the questions beat out of them.

I hiss with horror at that, and when the men lead the row of girls toward the door that goes into the basement, I make for my own door on silent feet. I run down the hallway, staying near the edge to avoid the creaky boards and dodging around the old pictures on the walls. Within moments I've reached the chute my father likes to use for laundry and jerked the door up, using the latch to secure it. I stare down into the darkness, my breathing heavy and my heart hammering. This chute leads to the laundry room in the basement, and is the quickest way from my room on the third floor to an exit.

I know, because I've used it before.

I also know that my body will fit into the chute, while larger men–like the ones my father employs–can't fit.

What I don't know is what the hell I'm doing. I've seen the

vans before, even seen the rows of girls filing into the basement's exterior door. But that's the extent of my knowledge. I've never asked, never even considered asking, where they might be going or what those girls are here for.

But I'm tired of not knowing. I'm tired of the whispers in this house, and the aura of evil around my father.

Those girls aren't much older than me. And they're not here of their own volition.

I want to know what the hell is going on.

I slip into the chute without putting any more thought into it, and reach back for the door. One jerk, another scuffle, and I'm shooting downward, my hands and feet held against the side of the chute to stabilize me. Three floors down, I emerge into one of the large baskets the maids put here for laundry, and freeze, listening closely.

In the distance, the murmur of voices. A door opening. A man threatening someone.

A girl sobbing, and the sound of a fist hitting bone. Sudden silence.

It's far away, though, and I don't think there's anyone in this room. They're putting them in one of the other rooms, further along the passageway that runs against the wall of the house here in the foundation.

Perfect.

I jump out of the laundry and rush for the door, opening it just far enough to see through. And then I nearly recoil in horror. The girls are filing right past me, and now that I can see their faces, I know I've done the right thing. They're bruised and broken, their expressions dead. Every so often, I see one crying quietly, but they're rare.

These girls aren't just beaten into submission. They've disappeared inside themselves, trying to escape reality.

I bite my lip, my young mind tearing through the possibilities as I try to figure out what's going on here. Are they prisoners? Slaves of some sort? I know New Orleans was once part of the south, and therefore a major port for the slave trade, but that's been finished for years. What are these girls doing here?

What is my father doing to them?

I latch onto that question and lose focus on the girls for a moment, and in that one moment of not paying attention, everything goes wrong. Another eye appears in the crack I'm looking through, and then the door is shoved open and I'm flying backwards. Rough hands and a furious face. A shouted question about who I am and what I think I'm doing, and then a promise that he's going to take me to my father.

He grabs me and hauls me up, then out into the hallway where I'm dragged past the broken girls, my screams hoarse and terrified. But the man is enormous and I'm small, and no matter how much I claw at him, he won't let me go. Before I know it, we're on the first floor and the door to my father's office is opening. I'm shoved through and fall to my stomach on the floor.

And when I look up, my father looks coldly calculating, and I know I never should have gotten out of my bed or gone to the basement. I shouldn't have tried to play hero for those girls.

Not when I can't even save myself.

I jerk myself out of the memory and turn my face up to the rain, my breath ragged and my stomach churning. I'm not in New Orleans. I left my father's house a long time ago, and he can't get to me now.

These days, I would kill him if he tried.

That's evidently the thought I needed to pull me out of my doldrums, because suddenly my brain is turned back on. I'm not in this crumbling apartment for kicks. I'm here because we just came out of the battle with the Poffo and Massimo tribes, and the city is in chaos. The Rossis are in charge, sort of, and the Brennans are at their side, but we didn't come through it without problems. Joseph was shot, Dante was kidnapped–and then saved–and Dax, our new ally and Dante's new silver fox, is recovering from injuries he sustained during the battle.

From his own cousin.

And me?

Sure, I stepped in and saved the day, thanks to my contacts in New Orleans. I showed up with the army Joseph and Michael Rossi needed, and we killed everyone in our path. But going home to get that help did something to me. I stepped out of the airport in New Orleans, into that thick, flower-scented air, and felt the New York version of Brooks Peterson crumbling away, like a disguise I couldn't maintain when faced with my history.

The Big Easy reached right into a chest of emotions I like to keep locked, and started pulling out ghosts. And now that those ghosts are out and screaming through my head, I don't know how to put them back in their chest again.

I shake myself and try to find the confidence I had a moment ago. I'm not that New Orleans version of Brooks anymore. I'm not Brooks Landry. I'm Brooks Peterson, most powerful woman in New York. I can handle anything that comes my way, and I always look good doing it.

I can save anyone who needs saving.

Christ, it's the main reason I avoided New Orleans for so long. Down there, I was powerless. At the mercy of the men who ran the city.

Up here, I'm the one who runs the show.

A beep interrupts my mental pep talk and I glance down at my phone, already annoyed. Lucien. Of course. He wants to talk. Of course. But as far as I'm concerned, he can go right on with waiting, because I don't have anything to say to him. Sure, he came to my rescue in New Orleans, and then loaned me the men I needed to save my friends. And he might be my ex-fiancé and the one man I thought I might actually love.

But I ran away from all of that years ago, and he didn't exactly follow me. He knew where I was–everyone knew–and he didn't come for me. He let me go, like none of it had mattered. And on the days when I'm being honest, I can admit that I've never gotten over how much that hurt.

So no, he doesn't have the right to pester me.

Especially now, when I'm still in the middle of a war.

And when I'm hearing rumors that girls are starting to disappear from amongst our ranks.

The thought takes me back to those dark vans on the street, and I glance down again, wondering. I don't know anything more than shadows of stories, and it's not enough to go on. It probably doesn't have anything to do with me or our war.

But it's awfully hard to hear that girls are disappearing and not think of my father and the smuggling ring I've always suspected he was running.

Runs.

Awfully hard not to connect those dots.

Nearly impossible, in fact.

I'm interrupted by my phone actually ringing, and this time when I look at it, ready to reject another of Lucien's calls, I'm surprised to see Camille's name instead. My cousin and best New Orleans friend, she almost never calls, because I almost never answer.

If she's calling, she has a good reason.

"Are you okay?" I ask, in lieu of a hello.

"I'm fine," she says, a smile caught up in her drawling voice. "But I have a message for you. Lucien says he's in town and you made him a promise. He also says he's got something you need."

Something I need. I almost snort. He doesn't have the first idea about what I might need right now. He doesn't even know why I was involved in a war on the streets of New York, or why we didn't have the soldiers to fight it on our own.

I almost tell Camille off for passing messages for someone like Lucien Boudreaux, because it's beneath her. But I catch myself before the words come out of my mouth. Because the thing about Lucien is that he knows things he shouldn't know. He has plans no one else understands, and contacts that make him invaluable.

If he's telling Camille he has something I need...

The problem is, he might not be lying.

And I can't take the chance of calling his bluff. Not until I know.

"Christ," I breathe.

Camille, that bitch, just laughs her breathy laugh, tells me to call her when I have time, and hangs up.

And I spin toward the apartment, trying to figure out whether I should get in touch with Lucien... or go about my business and make him go to the trouble of finding me, instead.

2

BROOKS

"**D**oes Sloane know you're here?"

I almost punch him for even asking, but stop myself just in time.

After all, Duca de la Roca is a friend, and Joseph Rossi's right-hand man. Not exactly someone you punch just because you're having a hard day. A hard week.

A hard fucking month.

He's also not the sort of person you tell about the hard month, though, so I keep my mouth shut on that score and settle for giving him the most withering glance I can manage on short notice.

"I'm going to pretend you didn't just ask that, Duca. Stop fooling around. What do you have for me?"

The man has the nerve to stare at me like he actually doubts me, and I turn away from him, already tired of the game. If he's going to play hard to get, I'm going to take the time to make sure I wasn't followed when I came in here. The bar is slick and sleek, everything you'd expect from a bar on the roof of one of the swankiest buildings in Manhattan. Chromed-out furniture with dark purple leather on the details. Glass tables with rusted steel supporting the clear surfaces, and a floor that's so black it looks like it must be hiding something sinister. The crowd here is equally shiny, a mix of girls too young to be out and men too old to be looking at girls like this. Dark suits and scowls on the men, while the girls are in candy pinks and bright oranges. Lipstick and pigtails and high heels. Loud music and laughter, and alcohol flowing like it's fucking water.

I don't have to ask to know this is one of Michael Rossi's bars. Everything about it screams money and decadence, and though he isn't a glittery person himself–far from it–he is an awfully good businessman. And he knows what the Manhattan crowds like.

Seeing as how it's Michael's, I guess the security is pretty good in here, but I'm not taking any chances. I watched the road behind me like a hawk on the way here and didn't see any cars that raised the hair on my neck. But that doesn't mean I didn't pick up a tail.

Hell, one of the reasons we chose the bar at all is the way it's set up. From where we're sitting–a booth at the back, that gives us at least a little bit of privacy–we can see the one and only entrance to the place. And there's so much noise in here that any casual observer would have trouble overhearing us.

Of course, Duca hasn't given me anything worth overhearing. Yet.

I reach for the Sazerac in front of me, hating that the New Orleans special was the first drink I thought of when I got here, and turn to Duca again. "Are you going to give me what I asked for or not?" I ask sharply. "Because if you just wanted to get me out on a date, there are easier ways to do it."

That gets a smile out of the man, and I grin in response. Duca is one of the best people I know, and would sell his soul for any of the Rossi clan–or Sloane, or Penny, or even me–but he almost never smiles. He also doesn't do side jobs that Joseph doesn't know about, though, and I was surprised when he called me and said he had information for me.

Because no, Sloane doesn't know I'm here, and neither does Joseph. At least, not technically. As the best fixer in the city, I very rarely tell my clients how I go about fixing their problems, and right now Sloane is my client, not my friend.

And I'm not sure, yet, whether I can fix the problem she presented me with.

But when she told me what happened, I knew I had to try. Partially because it dovetailed with what I was already doing.

The smile melts off Duca's face and he finally leans in like he's ready to get down to business. I put my drink down and lean in as well, unexpectedly nervous.

"What exactly are you hoping I'll give you?"

This time, I have to clench my fists to keep from hitting him. "I already told you what I want."

"But you didn't tell me why."

I snort. "Duca, have I ever told you *why* about anything I asked for?"

This is the truth, and he knows it. Duca might not be in the Rossi leadership yet, with Fat Jimmy still ruling the operation and Joseph a mere underboss, but he's high enough that he always has access to whatever information, weapons, and money the family has. Joseph trusts him with his life, and that means that if Joseph knows something, Duca does, too. He's always been my first call when I needed something no one else could get me.

Right now, that's more information about Sloane's missing cousin, Aislyn.

Logically, anything Duca knows will already have gone to Joseph, and from there to Sloane. Logically, my best friend already knows everything Duca is about to tell me. But Sloane herself–and therefore Joseph, and therefore Duca–don't know what I do about New Orleans or the deals they do for girls down there.

And I'm not exactly going to tell them.

But I need to know whether their information matches with my suspicions.

I need to know whether I have any shot at fulfilling Sloane's plea that I find her cousin.

Duca watches the thoughts flick across my face, though I'm working hard to keep them hidden, and finally nods.

"Right. I'll tell you what we know, but it's not much. Aislyn has been missing since the day of the battle. She went out to walk her dog in the morning and never came home again. No one knows what that means, of course. She could have decided she wanted a different life. Run off with a man. Could be playing some sort of game."

"But that's not Aislyn," I say quietly. I don't know the girl well, as she isn't mixed up in the mob side of Irish Brennan's family. She's his sister's daughter, and they've always kept her far from the blood and corruption of his life. But I know enough about her to know she's blond, very pretty, and very well-mannered. She doesn't do things she isn't supposed to, and never talks back to her parents.

In short, she's Sloane's polar opposite.

And she wouldn't disappear unless someone had taken her.

"That's not Aislyn," Duca agrees quietly, his eyes flitting around the bar. "Which is why everyone is worried. But there's more."

Of course there is. There's always more.

"She's not the only one who's gone missing," he continues. "Word is, a number of girls are suddenly disappearing. Girls who should have security around them. High-end families who can afford to keep their girls safe. Half of them are from mafia families. The other half are from society elite."

I almost drop the glass I'd picked back up. Mafia families. The society elite. Sure, there've been a couple of kidnappings lately–Sloane and Dante–but those are very specific to the war with the Poffo clan. Normally, the unwritten code of the Costa Nostra keeps women and girls safe from the wars. They don't disappear unless their own family disappears them, and that happens rarely.

A rash of girls suddenly disappearing is odd.

And it raised all the hackles on my neck, because it sounds all too familiar.

What the fuck is going on here? Girls are out of bounds, particularly when they're rich enough to have good security around them. And losing another Brennan...

We killed most of the Poffo men, and a good number of Massimos and Carusos, but the city is still in chaos as other families try to fill the power voids our war created, and now girls are being yanked off the streets. I'm starting to wonder whether we actually won the war, or if we just made everyone less safe.

Did I go all the way to New Orleans and open up that fucking closet of horrors, just to make New York even less stable?

As if on cue, my phone buzzes, rattling the table, and I grab at it, my nerves on high alert. One glance at the screen tells me that it's Lucien again. Like he heard me thinking about him or something.

Heard me doubting the move I made to bring him and his men up here to help me fight my battles.

You owe me, Brooklyn, the text reads.

I snarl at the phone and drop it back on the table. He isn't lying–I do owe him, and I made a promise–but I'm getting really tired of him rubbing my face in it. I'll pay up when I'm ready, and only if I decide it's what I want to do. I always pay my debts, and I never desert my friends. But he's asking the world, wanting me to move back to the Big Easy, and I'm not ready to think about it yet.

I also don't know whether I trust him.

I don't trust men in general. I did, after all, grow up with my father. And I saw how hard my mother fought to break free of him, packing up and leaving in the middle of the night with me in tow. Running for New York and her family here, like we had demons on our tails.

We had the devil after us. My father.

And I've never forgotten it. It's why I got here and changed my life. I worked hard to make the right friends and find us the security we needed. These days, I know how to take care of myself and get shit done without anyone else's help. Lucien's asking me to change that.

And I don't know if I can.

Even if seeing him again makes me feel as though my heart's breaking into a million pieces and he's the only one who can put it back together.

"Something wrong?" Duca asks, starting at me with suspicion all over his face.

"No," I snap too quickly. "What else do you have?"

He presses his lips together like he doesn't believe me–fair– but I stare at him until he keeps talking, unwilling to give up my secrets. What would I say? My father promised me to a boy I already loved, and when I figured out it was all a scam, I ran for New York and never looked back? And that boy is in town now trying to make me move home, and my heart is half on his side?

I don't think so.

"We're wondering," he finally continued, "if the Poffo and Massimo clans are running a new racket."

I pause for a beat. "But we killed them all."

He gives me a long look that says more than his words. "Did we?"

Shit.

"A kidnapping racket," I say. It's not a question. It's a statement.

Because I already know what those look like. I've been in the middle of one. And I was beaten nearly to death for discovering it.

"A kidnapping racket," he agrees quickly. "And not only here. My contacts tell me girls are disappearing in other cities as well. Las Vegas. Atlanta. Boston. New Orleans. Aislyn, if she's a victim, isn't the first. They're pulling from some of the biggest families. Even the Landry and Boudreaux clans down in New Orleans, and we all know how crazy you'd have to be to mess with them. But this time, they've pulled someone from one of the biggest families in New York. No one wants to let it stand. But no one knows where to start."

I'm up and moving before he finishes speaking, because my nerves won't let me sit there any longer. I toss a thanks over my shoulder to a confused Duca and then wind my way quickly through the crowded bar. Girls see me coming and get out of the way, their high heels slipping on the deep black floor. Men in suits take one look at me and scowl like they want to say something, but then decide it's not worth it.

Smart, I think.

Because the Glock in my shoulder holster and the blade in my pocket are the only answers they'd get.

I was hoping Duca had the information I need, but I hadn't realized how much he was going to give me. It's not just New York. It's every city where the mafia has a foothold.

Including New Orleans.

And they're taking girls who should be safe, from families who should be able to protect them.

Including my family.

I almost laugh at how Duca said it. The Landry and Boudreaux clans, like they're people I've never heard of. Names I might not even know. He doesn't realize who I am. No one here knows that I'm the Landry heiress, hiding in plain sight on the streets of New York and masquerading as nothing more than Brooks Peterson.

We hid up here so my father couldn't find us, and changed our name so no one would turn us in.

But now that I know pieces of what's going on–now that I know Aislyn isn't the only girl who disappeared–I feel my Landry blood rising to the surface once again. That deep, dark rebel who never really died down. The girl who, at thirteen, tried to save a group of victims before she knew what she was doing.

I couldn't save them then. But if that shit is still going on, I'm not going to stay in New York and hide from it.

This time, I'm going to stop it.

I just need to see proof that it is what I think it is.

I storm into the elevator and shoot a venomous look at the other inhabitants. They scatter through the doors like I've just held a gun to their head, and I grin to myself. Then I get to thinking about my next step. I told Sloane I'd find her cousin, and if Aislyn has fallen into the hands of traffickers, I'm pretty sure I know exactly where to start.

New Orleans has been a port rife with human trafficking since before the Civil War. If I was going to start smuggling people, that's the first place I'd go.

Which means I am going home. Just not for the reason Lucien Boudreaux wants.

I leave the elevator when it hits the ground floor and make my way quickly through the dark lobby toward the main doors, my mind flying ahead of me to make travel arrangements and figure out who I can count on in my old hometown. I'm no longer thinking about New York, or anyone here. I'm already in the dark, humid air of New Orleans, searching for a group of girls that needs saving.

Which is why I almost run into Lucien Boudreaux before I

see him, leaning against the door of a black sedan in a suit nearly as black as his fucking soul. He's all tousled brown hair and face as handsome as the devil, a cane at his side and his men surrounding the car behind him. He looks smooth and suave, as ever, and my first thought is that he should have been a pirate. Swashbuckling good looks that make you want to crawl into bed with him and do whatever he asks you to... and a tendency to sell anyone who gets too close.

My second thought is that he must be able to hear when I'm thinking about him and fly right to me. Maybe he's a fucking vampire rather than a pirate, with the ability to read minds and fly.

"Speak of the Devil, and he will appear," I breathe.

"Are you talking about me, love?" he drawls. "Because I was under the impression you were avoiding me, not summoning me. And I'm getting tired of waiting."

3

LUCIEN

God, she's beautiful.

It's been a week since I've seen her and I'd already forgotten the way she takes up all the air around her. The tip of her chin, as if she's waiting for the world to fall at her feet. The flash of that gaze, just daring anyone to get in her way. The face of an angel, with broad eyes and cheeks round enough to dimple when she smiles.

If you can get her to smile.

My hands clench at my sides with the memory of how soft that skin is, and the scent of her neck. Her hair. The spot right behind her ear.

I was in love with this girl, once. More than in love. I was going to marry her and spend the rest of my life with her, and I would have thanked God or Satan or the closest witch doctor every day for putting her in my path and convincing our fathers that our marriage was the best way to an alliance. I would have held her and protected her for the rest of my fucking days.

If she'd stuck around and let me do it.

Now...

Now I remind myself that she's not just beautiful but also a she-devil. Dangerous. Reckless.

Annoying.

I watch her storm in my direction, her face covered by a glare, and can't stop the smile that creeps over my lips. Or the way my cock is suddenly pressing against the zipper of my trousers. Because my brain might remember her beauty and danger, but my body remembers something else entirely. Something hot and reckless in a dark closet we weren't supposed to be in, with people strolling along outside the door and my hand over her mouth.

I can't help it. I've always liked dangerous things. And Brooks Landry is the most dangerous creature I've ever met.

I don't move to greet her, though. Because I've been following her for the last week, intent on bringing her to heel after the promise she made me, and now that I've finally found her, I'm not going to make it easy on her.

This time, I'm going to force her to come to me.

"You," she hisses, drawing to a stop right in front of me.

"Me," I agree easily. "Were you expecting someone else?"

Her eyes flash to the cane at my side, and she smirks. "Not really. Finally admitting your age, Lucien? Or is that just a fashion statement?"

I nearly laugh at that. Classic Brooks: right to the offensive. I managed to catch her by surprise and now she's trying to get her footing back. I don't rise to the bait, though. Not with words.

Instead, I grab the handle of the cane and jerk, pulling the hidden blade out of the body of the walking stick and swishing it quickly through the air. Once. Twice. When it stops, the tip of the steel is at the base of her neck.

"Fashion statement," I growl.

Her eyes move from the blade at her throat to my own, shocked and almost laughing, and before I can say anything else she's moving, quick as a cat and twice as sharp. A butterfly knife appears in her hand and snaps open, then whirs through the air to clash with my own blade and toss it away from her.

"What is this, League of Extraordinary Gentlemen? Because you're no Dorian Gray," she murmurs. "It's not about the size of the sword, Lucien. It's how you use it that matters." She flips her butterfly knife closed again, exaggerating the movement, and tosses me what can only be called a smirk.

I'm about to answer when my phone rings, and when I see Daniel's name, I take the call. Some things are more important than putting Brooks in her place.

"Boss," he says quietly.

My lips twitch. Daniel Boniface is my second, and my best friend, and takes his job very seriously. But he never calls me 'boss.' The term must mean he's with someone he's trying to impress. "Daniel. What's going on?"

"You need to get home. Things down here are... not going well."

The smile drops off my lips. "You're going to need to be more specific, Daniel." Because there are a range of things that aren't going well right now. A quiet war in New Orleans between some of the most powerful families, including my own. Shady deals that never see the light of day. The Big Easy has always believed in a less organized version of organized crime, and when I left a week ago, it had reached a truly disturbing level of chaos.

I need to know whether there's anything new.

As usual, Daniel gets straight to the point. "More girls missing. Some of them from families we know. Many of them from the same classes we've already guessed at. Word is, whoever's taking them is expanding to other cities, too. Word is, they're coming for specific families."

And now I'm flat out scowling. Not new, then, but definitely more serious than I realized. He's talking about the sudden rash of kidnappings in New Orleans. Girls are disappearing right and left down there, and there's no rhyme or reason to it. No patterns, and nothing I can see that connects the victims. The thing is, this isn't a new phenomenon–we've heard rumors about sex trafficking in the city before–but it's escalating. In the past, my sources told me there were shipments of 'inventory' coming through our port. Girls being shuffled from one ship to another in the dead of night as they made their unwilling way to the cities where they'd serve new masters in the sex trade.

But they weren't girls from our city. At least not that we could discover. They'd been from other cities and countries, brought through the New Orleans port because it was conveniently understaffed when it came to law enforcement. And they'd never been my problem.

My family didn't deal in flesh. We ran weapons and owned clubs, making our money from guns and cards, the way nature intended.

We would never have touched people. And we certainly wouldn't sell them.

But when girls we knew started disappearing as well, I started to ask questions. Unfortunately, I hadn't had the contacts to make quick progress in that world, and I was still in the process of breaking the walls they'd erected around that operation.

Then Brooks turned up in New Orleans, asking for my help in some war she'd started in New York–or maybe one that she just wanted to finish–and I'd put my New Orleans affairs on ice, leaving Daniel to continue the research.

If what he's saying is true, I'm overdue for getting back. I have friends who need saving.

And a friend here who doesn't yet know what sort of danger she's in.

"You made me a promise," I tell Brooks, ending the call with

Daniel. "If I came to help you finish your war, you'd come home. And yet you're still in New York."

She makes a face at me. "Promises extracted under duress don't hold any weight, Lucien, and you know it."

I finally take a step toward her, and then another, bringing my body close enough that I can feel the heat coming off her. Smell her perfume, and the scent of the absinthe on her lips. Sazerac. Of course she was up there drinking Sazerac.

She still has more New Orleans in her than she'd like to think.

I lean in and turn my face down into her neck, inhaling the deep amber scent of her skin, and then lift my hand to run a thumb over her lower lip. Straightening up, I find her deep blue gaze and press my tongue to the pad of my thumb.

The tang of licorice greets me, with an undercurrent of rye whiskey and bitters.

"Sazerac?" I ask. "I didn't know you still drank it."

Her eyes go wide and dark and she stiffens. "I don't," she whispers too quickly.

Her response sends fire scorching through my veins. Christ, this woman. Get too close and my need for her is already taking over. I take her chin between my fingers to hold her still, and brush my lips gently against hers, reveling in the tremors that run through her body. "And yet I can taste it on your lips and smell it on your skin. You're a terrible liar, Brooks Landry."

For a moment, the air between us is so thick you'd need a knife to cut through it, and I nearly take another step toward her, just to feel the brush of her body against mine. My cock is straining in my pants, fighting to get to her, and my skin feels as if a million razorblades are slicing into it.

Devils, just being around her makes my body forget everything my brain has learned.

Suddenly she jerks away from me, though, taking three steps back and tipping her chin up. "You don't know anything about me, Lucien. Not anymore. And my name isn't Landry. It's Peterson."

Her words douse whatever tension I might have been feeling, and I get down to business.

"I know a hell of a lot more than you think I do, Brooks, and it's time you started listening. If you'd taken any time to ask what I was doing in New Orleans when you showed up, you'd know that things aren't going well down there. Wars are being fought that could change the city."

"Hard to ask for news when I was busy running for my life," she retorts.

This time I do grab her, then spin and pin her against the car. I'm suddenly furious at everything. The fact that she was promised to me and then left like it didn't matter. The lack of any news after that.

The way she never called to tell me she was safe.

And then she showed up in New Orleans asking for help like I somehow owed it to her, expecting me to play hero, and I'd fucking done it. Marshaled my men and laid an army at her feet, like some god-cursed suitor begging for her hand in marriage.

Which was exactly what I'd been. I'd sold my own family out to come to her rescue, on the promise that if I did it, she'd come home with me. Only to fight the battle and then have her disappear into the darkness like fucking smoke.

Now Daniel is calling me telling me things are going badly in New Orleans, with more girls disappearing and families I know losing people, while I'm up here waiting for Brooks Landry to remember how to keep a fucking promise. I'm the Boudreaux heir and no one ever disrespects me. If they do, they find themselves dead in no time flat. Yet here's Brooks, pulling on my heart strings the way she always has and asking me to help her, then going back on her word the moment she changes her mind.

Breaking promises and putting herself in danger. And this

time, if my sources are right, she's up against something I'm not sure I can save her from.

She just doesn't know it yet.

"This isn't a joke, Brooks," I growl, getting as close to her as I dare. "I don't know what you think you're playing at, but you're already in over your head. All this research you're doing? The missing girls, and that girl you're searching for by name? The fucking war I came here to fight for you? You think that's not connected? You think it's some sort of coincidence?"

Now she finally lets her expression show something. "What?" she asks sharply. "What are you talking about?"

My hands clench on her arms. God, for such a smart girl, she can be really dense. "I'm talking about the case you're on right now. The girl, Aislyn Brennan."

Confusion slashes through her gaze, followed by defiance, and then anger. "How do you know about her?"

There are a million answers to that question, but only one of them matters. "Because I've been following you since I got here. And because the people you're talking to are passing word along to their keepers."

She shoves me off, now, that temper of hers getting the better of her, and glares at me. "And what the fuck does *that* mean?"

"It means," I tell her coldly, "that according to my sources, they're involved in something a lot bigger than you realize, and they don't like you poking around. They've put a hit out on you. You've been asking too many questions, and now they're after you, too. And these aren't the sort of people you can run from, because they'll find you. No matter where you hide."

She opens her mouth, no doubt with some other smart-ass question, but snaps it shut when the first bullet flies our way.

4

LUCIEN

I duck on instinct, then fly forward and grab Brooks on my way into a roll. We hit the concrete in a ball, my body tucked around hers to cushion it, and the moment we come up we're running toward the black SUV. I don't look for my men. I don't even wonder whether they're safe or not. They have their own car, and one responsibility.

Protect Brooks.

I told them when we arrived that our meeting might be interrupted, and if it was, that their job was to make sure Brooks got out of there safely. I could handle myself, I said, and they all know it's the truth.

Looks like I'm handling Brooks as well, though, because I'm not willing to leave her to whichever of my men are still around. She's too important. I dash toward the car, her hand in mine and her body echoing my movements. The girl's got the instincts of a cat, though I already knew that. She doesn't stop to ask stupid questions about who's shooting at us or why. She's running like she already knows what's going on.

Like we've been doing this together for years.

Devils, we should have been. If there was any justice in the world, we would have been married years ago and living as partners in crime down in New Orleans.

A bullet whistles past my ear and hits the SUV, and I put thoughts of our past to the side. Now isn't the time to get riled up about Brooks having skipped town when we were supposed to get married. I'll take that up with her—again—once we're out of range of whoever's shooting at us.

"Who the fuck is shooting at us?" she snaps, breaking away from me and running for the passenger door while I jump into the driver's seat.

I hit the ignition and shove the car into reverse, waiting only seconds for her to find her seat. Then I jam my foot down on the gas and swerve off the curb, moving backward away from our other car. My men are crouched behind it, shooting madly at the line of vans coming down the street.

The flashes of gunfire from those vans tell me there are at least ten men in there with guns, though. I only brought five men. Good ones, but I'm not gambling on them being able to take out the vans. We have to get the fuck out of here.

I spin the wheel while we're still moving, sending us into a steep turn, and then jam the car into first and hit the gas again. Second. Third. Soon we're going 50 down a residential street in New York, and I'm trying to remember where we are and how to get out of here.

"Remember how I said you had a hit out on you?" I snap, eyes on the rear view. My men are holding the line, but one of the vans smashes right through their gunfire and is on our tail. And based on how they're driving, they're a lot less concerned about potential pedestrians than I am.

Fucking devils.

"How would they even know I was here?" she snaps, her hands busy on the gun she pulled from somewhere.

I pause for a moment, wondering where the hell she had it.

She's dressed in tight jeans and an even tighter top, and she doesn't have a bag. Where the hell had she stuffed a gun?

Probably the same place she had that fucking knife, I realize.

Maybe she had a secret compartment built right into her body. It wouldn't surprise me.

"They have sources better than you can imagine," I reply. "Better than you and me put together. The guy you were talking to is probably one of theirs."

She snaps a magazine into her gun and cocks it, and I can feel her gaze burning a hole into my cheek. "No. Duca is all Rossi. He'd never sell me out."

I don't know who this Duca is, but the fact that he's a man makes me immediately hate him. Who is he to Brooks, and how does she know he's so loyal? Was that who she was meeting with up there? In that swanky, sparkly club with all the drugs and booze?

I'll kill him.

Though that's not my problem right now, the voice in my head whispers. Focus on driving. Focus on living. Worry about Brooks' man—men—once you're safe.

Fucking voice, always being right.

"Well someone did," I respond. "Someone's been reporting what you've been doing. I don't know who, and I don't know who they're reporting to. But they're bigger than the Rossis. Bigger than your family or mine."

She stops what she's doing long enough to stare at me. "And how the fuck do you know that?"

I reach out and grab her wrist, turning to stare at her despite the fact that we're now going 50. "Because things are going badly in New Orleans, and I've been trying to figure out what's going on. And your name has come up in places I shouldn't be seeing it. Multiple times."

Her face goes slack with shock for a moment. "And why would you care about that?" she whispers.

Because I love her.

Because I've loved her since she was twelve and I was sixteen and we met on a playground where I was running cons. And when I think she might be in trouble, I will stop at nothing to save her.

I don't say any of that. Instead, I glance quickly at the gun she's holding and toss her the one I keep strapped to my chest. "That doesn't matter, love. There's a van following us and I don't know how many men are in it. Shoot for the tires and the engine and get them off our tail so I can get you back to my hotel."

She takes my gun, ejects the magazine, and checks that it's full in such a smooth set of motions that I almost don't see it. When she slams the magazine home again, she shakes her head.

"Not your hotel. Get to Brooklyn. Head for the Rossi brownstone."

Then she turns, breaks through the window with the butt of the gun, and leans out like she does this sort of thing all the fucking time. She's shooting before she gets all the way out, the gun booming with each shot, and I spare her one glance, then jump on the gas of the car and send it speeding down the street. The street is wide here, and mostly empty thanks to the late hour, but there are too many fucking cars parked along the side and I don't have as much room as I want. I swerve around a car that's parked too far out, then jerk the wheel and swerve in the other direction to avoid some other guy who's decided now is a good time to cross the street. Once I'm clear of him I slam my foot on the accelerator and ask the car for greater speed. Behind us, the van on our tail is shooting with what sounds like multiple tommy guns and I cock my head, wondering what's going on.

No modern gun would give that rat-a-tat sound. Even machine guns sound more like explosions at this point.

What did they do, bring antique guns to the fight? They're

sophisticated enough to be running a multi-city trafficking ring and yet they're shooting at us with–

The back windshield explodes and I duck instinctively, then reach over, grab Brooks by the back of her blouse, and jerk her back into the car.

"What are you doing?" she gasps. "I just got a bead on the driver!"

"And they're close enough to shoot out the back window of the fucking car," I snap. "Which means they're close enough to shoot you. We're done with that project. Time to run."

She splutters something about doubting whether I'm up to the task, but I'm not listening. I turn the wheel and take us into a spin, using every inch of the street for the slide and praying we're going to make it.

We don't.

We're turned almost all the way around when I realize that we don't actually have enough room and yank the wheel the other way, trying to regain control of the vehicle. It doesn't work, though, and we hit one of the parked cars, the door on Brooks' right crumpling with the sound of metal dying. Brooks is jerked to the right, but I grab her before she can fly out of the window. I jam on the gas again and the car tears away from the truck it just hit, metal screeching in protest as we fly away. We pass the van that was following us and I have enough time to look over and see the driver looking at me, his mouth open and his eyes wide with shock.

Brooks shoots through my window and hits him right between the eyes before he can try to follow us, though, and my last look at him tells me that he's already dead. His eyes are blank and his mouth hangs open with the weight that only death can bring.

I don't pause. I put his picture into my memory for later and tear up the street, trying to remember how the fuck to get back to my hotel from here.

And wondering whether any of my men are still alive.

***

B rooks still hasn't said anything to me when I come to a sharp halt in the circular driveway of my hotel. I look up and see the valet looking at us, but wave him sharply off.

Usually I'd be all for having someone else park my car. But I need to deal with the angry woman in my passenger seat first. And come up with a story for why I have broken windows, spent bullet casings, and guns lying around a car that needs to go back to the rental agency.

"I don't need your help, Lucien," Brooks says suddenly, breaking her silence.

I turn to her, wondering if she's finishing a conversation she's been having in her brain. Because I don't know what the hell she's talking about. Still...

"The past twenty minutes seem to prove otherwise," I snap.

She sneers at that. "And I could have taken care of them on my own if you'd given me the chance."

I reach out, grab her wrist, and yank her toward me. "You would have been killed if you were on your own. Or worse, kidnapped. Don't be stupid, Brooks."

She looks up at me, her eyes dark in the fluorescent lighting coming from the shelter above us, and swallows heavily. "And why would you care about that? It's been a long time since I was any of your business."

I almost laugh, because it's such a ridiculous thing to say. I don't, though, because I'm too busy trying to breathe around her scent. Trying to remember that I'm angry with her, and use that against the way my body wants to pull her into my lap and remind her of what we once had. "Except a week ago, you showed up in New Orleans asking for my help again. And that makes this situation my business. You might not be, but the war is," I say quietly.

She douses the tension as quickly as it began. "So you admit that I'm not your problem."

Right. Same old Brooks. I can need the girl like the air I'm breathing, but she'll never admit to needing me back.

And I'd be a fool to expect anything else.

I shake off the feelings that had been growing in my chest and reach into the pocket on the door, then toss the file I find there onto her lap. "The file of everything we found on the girls who are missing from New Orleans. Your friend's in there, too. Aislyn. Something is going on, and it started in New Orleans. You want to find her? Come home. Let me keep you safe while we figure this out. They're already on to you, and they're going to find you eventually. If they do, you're not going to be able to save anyone."

I close my mouth and let a beat pass, watching as she processes everything I've just told her.

"Let me help you, Brooks. Just this once."

She catches her lower lip in her teeth, and it's just about the sexiest thing I've ever seen. Not that I'm looking.

"I don't need your help."

I shrug. "So you've said."

"Are you going to get in my way?"

I smirk. "Define getting in the way."

She narrows her eyes, shooting sparks at me with those blue orbs, but snatches up the file I gave her. "This doesn't make us anything. And it doesn't mean I'm coming home for you."

And now I'm angry enough to be finished with the banter. "What makes you think I want to be anything with you?"

When she answers, I hear that she's angry, too—though I

don't know why. "Because I know you. And I know how you think."

She jerks on the handle of the door, having to try twice to get it open, and flies out of the car without a backward glance. I watch her go, eyes narrowed and mind tearing through all the possible implications of this situation. I came up here with the intention of bringing her home, not only for myself but to fulfill the contract that's been forced on me. I want her home with me, and thanks to that contract, I have to have her there. Regardless of how she feels about it.

But I don't want to do it this way. Taking her home angry... was never part of the plan.

Then again, I suppose I was stupid to expect anything with Brooks to go to plan. It almost never does.

And I'm just now realizing that I don't know her well enough anymore to be able to make plans that include her, anyhow. Not really.

Sort of like how she doesn't know me–or my motivations– nearly as well as she thinks she does.

5

BROOKS

The world outside is dark. Fathomless. Full of secrets. I don't know who's out there or what they want, and I'm not even sure what any of it has to do with me.

And I hate it. I've spent most of my adult life knowing exactly what I'm doing and who I'm dealing with, and on the rare times when I don't know, I always have one thing: I'm Brooks fucking Peterson, and I'll figure it out. I always have plan.

I always have a way out.

My eyes slide from the window, which shows nothing but darkness, to the man sitting across the aisle from me, and I cringe. I always have a way out until it comes to Lucien Boudreaux and the hold he's had on me since I was twelve.

He still has that hold on my soul, his sticky fingers reaching inside me and finding their way into my most private spaces.

And gods, do I hate him for it.

He's staring at me now, his dark eyes shuttered to keep me from seeing his thoughts, and it's all I can do to keep from jumping up and strangling him. First he shows up at the bar, saying he has business with me, then he virtually kidnaps me, gets me into a gunfight, and brings me to the airport rather than the Rossi mansion, which was where I wanted to go. Within half an hour of him picking me up, I found myself on his private plane at JFK, my head spinning at how quickly it happened.

Is that how it goes for all girls when they're kidnapped?

I wonder.

I've never been kidnapped myself, and though I have friends who have–Sloane and Dante both found themselves on the wrong side of a ketamine-soaked cloth in the last month–I haven't asked them if it happened so quickly they could hardly remember the details of it. I certainly haven't asked if they spent the entire journey fighting between burning love and ice cold hatred for the man kidnapping them.

My eyes go to Lucien again, and when I find him still staring at me, a slight smirk on that pirate's mouth of his, I drop my gaze to the file in my lap and start reading, determined to take my mind off the man. Research. Research is a good way to distract myself from the man who was once the love of my life.

Especially when that research might lead me to my current mark.

The world falls away from me at the thought, and my brain finally decides to get down to business.

The folder in front of me holds thirty files, at least, and on top is a sheet labeled 'Aislyn Brennan.' A glance at the picture shows me what I expected: A pretty girl, delicately blond and flushed. Freckles across her nose and bright blue eyes. The text to the side tells me her age–only twenty-three–and her family relations. Irish Brennan's niece. In graduate school for an English degree, with the dream of becoming a teacher. No boyfriend. Decent credit. One car and a flat that her parents bought her.

Nothing that stands out except that relationship with Irish, and her striking beauty.

And if I was a sex trafficker, the fact that she's young and looks untouched.

My stomach turns at that and I flip to the next file, and then the next. They're much the same. Girls that look young and pure, with an innocent beauty that sets your teeth on edge. None of them stand out as anything special or different, but they're all attached to prominent families. The Brennans in New York. The Boudreaux and Landry clans in New Orleans. A de la Roca, which means she may or may not be related to Duca. A Lafayette from New Orleans. Some names that I recognize as the Irish mob leaders in Boston. A few that say they're from Atlanta.

All related to mafia or mob families.

All young girls.

I slam the folder closed and shut my eyes, trying to get my brain to work. It doesn't make sense. Is there a collector out there, looking for girls who all fit this same mold? If there is, it doesn't follow that they've all been pulled from our world. There are plenty of pretty girls out there that don't come with the dangers of mafioso friends and relatives. Is someone specifically collecting girls from the underworld?

I pause and tip my head at that, wondering. It makes a certain sick sense. Men have eclectic tastes, particularly when they have too much money, and I can imagine someone wanting to collect girls who have mafia in their veins.

The bigger problem is the timeline. I know enough about trafficking rings like this to know they can't afford to hold girls for long. The longer they have them, the better the chances that they'll be discovered or killed. Two weeks, I think, horrified. And based on my surface-level knowledge, that's an outside figure.

If we're lucky, they keep the girls for two weeks before they ship them out. If we're unlucky, they only keep them a week.

And Aislyn has already been missing for three days.

"Found anything yet?"

I open my eyes to find that Lucien has moved into the seat across from me, gliding so silently that I didn't hear him coming. Made of smoke and shadows, that one. And mirrors that only show you what he wants you to see.

I don't trust him.

But I need to know what he knows.

"Why are they all the same?" I ask bluntly. "Young, pretty, untouched. There's nothing unique or interesting about any of them."

His mouth quirks. "They'd probably take offense to that, love."

"Don't call me 'love,'" I say, my stomach turning. "You lost that right a long time ago."

He presses his lips together and narrows his eyes at me, like he's weighing a number of possible responses to that, and I watch him warily. I've known Lucien Boudreaux since I was twelve. My mother and I had already escaped New Orleans by that time, moving to her family in the Irish enclave in New York, where we found shelter and sunshine after living in my father's dark, abusive world for too long.

My mother, however, in her somewhat scattered version of wisdom, had thought it was a good idea to take me back to the Big Easy twice a year to visit my father. I've never understood why she did it, and she's never been able to give me a good reason. Maybe it was some misbegotten idea that I should still know my father, even after she kidnapped me to get me away from him.

Maybe she just needed him to keep giving her a monthly check, and saw me as a sacrifice to keep him sweet.

Whatever the answer, I regularly found myself in New Orleans over my winter and summer breaks from school, always terrified of my father and counting the moments until I could return to New York. Until I was out shopping with my mother and cousin one day and saw the most beautiful boy I'd ever experienced. Dark hair and even darker eyes, tall and gangly in that way teenage boys are before they grow into their bodies, and yet somehow graceful, as if he knew exactly how to use himself. He was conning other kids at the park, cheating them out of their lunch money, and I watched him, fascinated at how quick his hands were, and how brilliant his smile. When he turned and caught my eye, we spent several moments staring at each other, our gazes clashing in a way that should have felt terrifying but was instead heavy with importance.

I know a lot of people don't believe in love at first sight, but when Lucien and I first laid eyes on each other, the world rearranged itself around us and laid a path that meant we would walk through life together.

We began finding ways to meet again and again, and two years after I first saw him I was leaning up against the wall of the library, his arms caging me in and his lips brushing against mine. Three years after that, I found out that my father and his had brokered a deal for an alliance, and the knot that tied it all, pun intended, was my marriage to Lucien.

I'd been brutally in love with him by that time, head over heels, and we'd been happier than I thought possible. I'd been looking forward to a future as the queen of the Boudreaux enterprise, and had spent more and more time in New Orleans just to be with Lucien.

Then I found out that my father had only brokered the deal to get a mole into the Boudreaux world so he could steal their rackets, and my world came crashing down. Moments after my father told me as much, I started to wonder whether Lucien was involved as well, and if he knew exactly what was going on. If it was a deal he'd agreed to for business reasons rather than the love I thought we had.

I'd already known I couldn't trust my father. My mother might have been empty-headed, but she taught me to recognize a man for what he was, and my father was my first test dummy. But when I started to doubt Lucien, my entire world had come crashing down and that had been the end of the engagement. I turned eighteen and started using my brain, and could see a range of potential reasons for Lucien to be lying to me about how much he knew. Power. Money. The alliance his father and mine wanted so badly.

It had taken no time for me to start seeing everything he did as suspicious, and within a month I skipped New Orleans and never returned.

I didn't say goodbye.

And he didn't come looking for me.

I swallow the sob that wants to emerge with that thought, the shooting pain of a knife twisting in my heart at how long I waited, certain that he was going to find me, and remind myself that the situation made me the new version of myself. I stopped waiting for men and began figuring out how to do things for myself. I stopped trusting people I didn't know.

I learned to handle everything with my own hands rather than counting on someone else.

And I put my heart and all its soft, squishy feelings to the side, along with my memories of Lucien Boudreaux. Because nothing good had ever come of trusting a man like that.

Now I give him my most charming smile, though, and wonder whether I can play off whatever feeling he still has left for me.

Lucien's eyes snap to the folder in my lap and then back up, his gaze clashing with mine. "What are you thinking?"

Ah, we've switched to Right to the Point Lucien, then.

That makes this easier.

"Probably nothing you don't already know. Too many girls are missing and it's been going on too long. We need to know who's taking them and why, and where these girls are ending up. Why are they focusing on girls who should be safe?

Where's their security when they're taken? Where are they being held?"

He nods once, his eyes going distant, then jumps to the next point I was going to make like he already knows where I'm heading. "And why are they going to other cities? If this started in New Orleans and comes down to a New Orleans family, why are they taking girls from Boston, Atlanta, and New York?"

His gaze sharpens on that last word, and I know he's thinking more than he's saying there, too.

Because he's guessed exactly what I'm thinking. He's just not saying it.

"And if Aislyn is the first girl taken in New York, why did they go right for a girl connected to my friends?" I ask quietly, letting my mind run through the implications. I don't know Aislyn personally, but that hardly matters. She's a Brennan, cousin to my best friend, and her disappearance comes on the heels of three families attacking the Brennans on what has always felt like a flimsy excuse. Sylvester Poffo and his under-lings, the Massimos and Carusos, came after the Rossi and Brennan families because Sylvester Poffo wanted more power in New York and thought he'd get it if he took out the largest fami-lies in the city. He paid the Massimos to attack the Rossi and Brennan organizations, and the Massimos hired the Carusos to do the dirty work.

Operationally, it makes sense.

As far as Poffo's motivations, though... I've never bought it. It feels too simple. Like something a high schooler would come up with, not a major player straight from Italy. I haven't had time to put too much thought into it, because we've been busy fighting a war, but now that I have a moment to breathe, my brain can't let go of the idea.

That excuse was too simple, and if it feels too simple and looks too simple, it usually is.

What if Poffo was working for–or with–someone else, and

attacked the Rossis and Brennans for reasons that had nothing to do with power in New York and everything to do with power somewhere else? And were those families truly a random target, or were they picked because that was where I found a home?

"I think you're right," Lucien says quietly.

I jerk back into the present and stare at him, trying to remember what we were even talking about. Did I say something that requires a response? Is he answering a question?

Or has he been watching me work through the problem without him?

"You don't even know what I'm thinking," I snap.

He chuckles, the sound dark and melty, and it trickles down my skin like hot syrup. Sticky. Impossible to get rid of.

"Your poker face isn't as good as you think it is, Brooks."

Now it's my turn to laugh, though it comes out shrill and awkward, which pisses me off. "My poker face is the best in the business, Lucien."

He shakes his head slowly and leans toward me, the air around us suddenly going so electric that the hairs on my arms standing up. His eyes drop to my lips and then rise back up so slowly that I can feel his gaze dragging over my skin. He's abruptly too close. Too big. Too male.

"Maybe to people who don't know you. But you forget. I grew up learning how to read you. You can't hide from me, love."

A fine shiver runs through my body, and I forget how to breathe for a moment. Lucien is all I can see, his woodsy scent filling my mouth and his eyes going so dark I feel like I'm drowning in them. He's right; he did grow up learning to read me. Any time I was in New Orleans, he claimed me and spent my days–and some of my nights–keeping me to himself. When we learned we were to be married, it had been a natural progression because we'd already been so wrapped up in one another.

But that was then and this is now, and he's wrong if he

thinks I'm still that lovesick little girl. He doesn't have the ties on me that he used to have. I cut them a long time ago, and swore that no one would ever hold me like that again.

"You don't know me as well as you used to. Things have changed."

He reaches out and runs a finger along my lower lip, his eyes following it like he can't look away, and all the blood rushes into my lower belly. I want to arch my back and take his finger into my mouth. Fall into the familiar rhythm we once had together and let him tell me exactly what we're going to do about all of this.

I don't want to be alone anymore.

But that's not the right answer, I tell myself firmly. Because I know better. I may not know what Lucien has been up to for the last ten years, but I do know one thing: When it comes to him, there are always traps. And you almost never see them before you find yourself falling.

Even now, I suspect that he knows more than he's telling me. I would bet that he came to New York with this information already in his pocket, ready to use it when the moment presented itself, as either blackmail or something more nefarious. Christ, there's even a chance he's involved in it. After all, his family is one of the most powerful families in New Orleans. They don't deal in smuggling, at least not that I know of, but Gemini Boudreaux is a brilliant businessman. If he saw an opportunity, I'm betting he would take it. And he'd drag Lucien along with him.

I admit to myself, very quickly, that I don't want to believe that. I don't want to think Lucien would ever enter sex trafficking. I'd like to believe that he has more humanity, more decency, than that. Because how could I ever have loved someone who would do something that horrific?

And what will I do if I find out he *is* involved?

Will I stand up to him and destroy him, the way I should?

Or will my heart get in the way and stop me?

I need to get my heart out of the equation, by hook or by crook, and the moment I have that thought, I know how to do it.

"Did you have anything to do with it?" I ask, counting on the question to be confusing enough for him to make a mistake and tell me the truth.

His expression shutters and he pulls his hand away from my mouth. "Anything to do with what?"

Dammit. Well, the truth, then. "My father's real reason for our marriage."

Lucien's face goes through a range of sudden changes, from confusion to understanding and then shock and anger. "His plan to put a mole into my family for information? Your idea that he was planting a spy rather than handing me a wife? No. Of course not. That doesn't even make sense."

He's right; it doesn't. It probably never did. But I was convinced at the time that Lucien had known what was going on and agreed to it.

"But it made sense at the time," I note. "Why else would you have agreed to marry me?"

"And why would I agree to a plot that would endanger my family?" he returns. He lays a gentle finger on my hand and shakes his head. "I wanted you, Brooks. That was my only thought." When I don't answer, he continues. "You should have come to me for answers. I would have helped you. Saved you from your father."

Now I do jerk away from him, furious at the idea that I needed saving.

Furious at the fact that he's right.

"You would have helped me for your own reasons, and they would have been just as bad as my father's. How long until we get to New Orleans? I want to find Aislyn and get back to New York, where things make sense."

He doesn't answer me this time, but gives me a long, weighted look, and then moves back to his original seat.

Good. I can't think when he's in my space, and right now, I need my brain more than ever. All my body wants is Lucien, and I need to keep my brain strong enough to overrule that urge.

Because Lucien is the last thing I need when I'm trying to save girls from a fate worse than death.

6

LUCIEN

The morning sun is just coming over the horizon when I walk out onto the balcony of my bedroom, coffee in hand and my mind full of questions. I glance up at the sky, mind still relaxed with sleep, and see that it'll be a beautiful day. No clouds in sight, and the chill of the morning gives me hope that we'll have cooler temperatures.

Good for doing some badly needed reconnaissance.

Because if my calculations are correct, we're running very short on time.

I go quickly through my mental notes, shuffling the pieces until I have a clear picture of where we were before I was–ahem–called to New York to help a 'friend.' I'd been hearing rumors about girls disappearing, and friends of ours were coming up missing. My sister lost her best friend and was working with me to make lists of the girls we hadn't seen in some time so I could check on their whereabouts. I'd heard rumors about a trafficking ring but didn't have anything solid, and was in the middle of trying to shore up my contacts. I'd even gone so far as to start asking pointed questions about trafficking and whether anyone in the city had their thumb in that pie, yet, or if it was a niche I could fill.

The memory of it makes me cringe. Everything about that world is dark and tainted, including the people who run it, and having contact with them–even through intermediaries–left a bad taste in my mouth. I'd felt as if I had a film of grime on me all the time, and the pictures I'd seen made me want to bleach my eyeballs.

Then Brooks showed up in New Orleans, all damsel in distress and speeding through the streets on what I thought was probably a stolen Ducati, and my red flags went up. When Daniel came to me and said she'd been spotted at the airport, I had to admit that part of me had been expecting it. I'd been edgy all evening, my skin itching as though I'd walked through something sharp, and it hadn't made sense. I was working on something I didn't like and the city was thick with intrigue and danger, but that was nothing new, and it shouldn't have brought my instincts to the surface. But I'd felt as though someone was standing behind me, whispering my name against my neck and then disappearing when I turned around to catch them.

For several moments, I'd entertained the suspicion that someone was playing a trick on me. Using voodoo to get under my skin. In a town like New Orleans, it's not as unbelievable as it sounds. I have a witch doctor on my staff for that very reason.

Then Daniel told me about Brooks being in town, and the pieces slid into place like a puzzle neatly finished off.

Of course she was. My body had always known when she was around, like she was a battery and I was her perfect match, attracted to her whenever she got near enough. She was the gravity to my moon, the pull to my push. My brain might not register her presence, but my instincts always did.

I'd also known she would come back, at some point. I just didn't know when–or why.

The thought takes my eyes down to the garden outside the

mansion, and I breathe out slowly. She's down there now, barefoot and drinking coffee like her life depends on it, her steps quick as she paces. She's in the rose garden, turning sharply around the bushes and muttering to herself, and I glance around the grounds, wondering if anyone else is there with her. The yard isn't big enough to hide anyone–nothing like the grounds of my father's mansion up the street–but it's well appointed. A wide lawn full of bright green grass, the rose garden, and a small outbuilding done in gray stone. A forested patch that features twisted magnolia trees and so much dripping Spanish moss that I wonder if I need to have someone out to take a look at it. The pool and hot tub, surrounded by hand-picked sculptures that match the gothic, Romanesque architecture of the house itself.

Some would call it overdone. Maybe even gaudy.

But to me, it's just home. New Orleans at its very base: gothic and built of stone and moss. Showy when it should be subtle, and hiding in plain sight. I bought the estate when I was only twenty-one and finally able to escape my father.

Brooks has never seen it. She was long gone by that time.

I pull my brain back to the leggy redhead currently wearing a path in my garden. She's agitated; that much is obvious. She's had more than enough coffee, if her actions are anything to go by, and if I know the girl, she's already planning something.

Probably something that will get her in trouble. She's always thought she was capable of more than any other human.

A smile touches my lips at the thought, and I glance at her face. She's frowning in concentration, and it makes her features even harder. She's gorgeous, but there's something sharp about her, like she'll cut you with her eyes if you get too close. Lithe and graceful, she's also poised for action, and one look at her quick fingers will tell you she's lethal. No man would survive a close encounter with her.

And holy devils, do I adore her.

I give in to the urge for just a moment, allowing that

emotion to run through me. I don't often give in to it–partially because I haven't seen her in so long–but here, in my own home where I don't need to maintain any masks, I can admit to myself that she's held my heart for longer than she realizes.

Not that I can trust her with it. She's run from me before without a backward glance, and I learned my lesson then. Brooks Landry isn't a girl to be trusted. She'll sell her soul for the people she loves, but getting into that inner circle is nearly impossible.

I put my emotions away and force cold, hard logic onto the problem. Brooks isn't here for me, anyhow. She's here to solve the mystery of where her friend's cousin has gone, and I'm not stupid enough to think I can stop her. Hell, I'm not even stupid enough to get in her way. I've seen her on a mission before, and once she has a direction, she won't change it. She'll sell every organ in her body to get it done, and kill anyone who tries to stop her.

Which makes it lucky, I guess, that for this moment, she and I want the same thing.

And as long as she's in town...

Well, I wouldn't be a man if I didn't take advantage of it, would I?

I put my coffee cup down, smile to myself, and saunter back into my room, the hazy idea of Brooks trapped in my house and at my mercy drifting through my head.

***

When I get to her, Brooks takes about half a second to start making demands.

"I need access to your network," she says abruptly, as if we're in the middle of a conversation I didn't know we were having. "I'll need all the files you have so I can start searching for Aislyn. And the name of anyone you've made contact with who knows anything."

I pull a cigarette from its pack and slide it into my mouth. "Don't ask for much, do you?"

She grabs the cigarette and tosses it over her shoulder. "This isn't a joke, Lucien. And stop smoking. It's terrible for your lungs. And your skin." She glances at me and lifts one brow. "Actually, that might be why you're looking so old these days."

"I'm not looking old," I say, caught off guard and strangely offended by the off-hand comment. "I'm only four years older than you!"

She kicks the cane out from underneath my hand and huffs. "And yet you look ancient and are using a cane. That doesn't say much for your health, old man."

I fall forward when the cane disappears–partially an act–and when I come up again, I'm close enough to feel every inch of her body against my own. Her breasts press against my chest, her nipples rock hard under the sheer blouse, and her hips fit neatly between my own, just as they always have. Brooks is tall for a woman but I'm taller, and I've got at least a full head on her these days. I put a finger under her chin and tip it up so she's looking at me, and her eyes go dark with something I don't recognize. Fear. Lust.

Expectation.

Something rears its head inside my chest, and I forget to move for several seconds with the force of it. I thought on my balcony that the house was home, but I was wrong. The house is a structure where I lay my head and find safety, but home? Real home? The security of knowing you've found a place here your soul will always belong, and where you can always feel safe?

That's staring up at me right now, barefoot and smelling of coffee and vanilla, her lips parted and hair still messy with sleep. Those eyes are the same ones that met mine when I was only sixteen and so intent on conning my friends that I hadn't even realized anyone was watching, until I looked up and found blond hair and blue eyes and a face so beautiful I'd thought I was dreaming.

She was home to me for so long that when she left, I tore the world apart trying to replace her.

That thought brings me back to my senses and I step away from her. She might have been home once, but that was a long time ago. These days, she's just a girl who needs my help and called on our history to secure it.

"You have a plan, then?" I asked, turning back to the conversation we started. To my annoyance, my voice comes out husky and full of something I don't dare name.

"Of course I do."

She grins at me, and it's the first time I've seen that smile in years. It does something strange to my stomach.

Something I don't like.

I narrow my eyes at her. "Of course? Why am I afraid that means it's a very bad, very dangerous idea?"

"Because it probably is. But it'll work. I just need access to your network. And your contacts. And transportation."

I shake my head. "No. You're not leaving here on your own. That's non-negotiable." It's out of the question, honestly. Now that she's here, I'm not letting her out of my sight. I might not trust her, and I certainly don't need her, but I would kill myself if anything happened to her. She can get in trouble on her own time. If she's with me, I'm going to keep her safe. Hard stop.

Her gaze narrows to match mine. "I'm not here as your captive, Lucien. I'm not going to play that game."

I lean forward and brush my lips over hers, unable to stop myself, and find her lips soft and coffee-flavored. Hotter than I could have imagined. Smooth and perfect. The kiss is a quick one, barely a brush, but when I pull away, I feel as if I've been branded.

The world is on fire. And I'm burning along with it.

"Not a captive," I breathe. "We'll call you a guest." I turn and start walking away, desperate to put some space between us, and toss the rest of my answer over my shoulder. "I'll get you access to the network. And I'll help you with your bad idea. But only because it happens to match with mine. Don't step out of line, Brooks, or I'll change my mind. Consider yourself warned."

7

BROOKS

I bust through the doors of the ridiculous mansion, the files clutched to my chest and a thumb drive in my pocket.

That was easier than I expected it to be, and I take a moment to grin to myself. After our little meeting in the garden, where Lucien tried to not only sweet talk me but also intimidate me–neither of which worked–I went into the house, showered and changed in the suite he gave me, and then went to find him in his office. He'd promised me access to his network and contacts, and I didn't want to wait.

If the timeline I have living rent-free in my head is right, Aislyn could only have three more days before she's shipped to wherever they're sending her. If she's been kidnapped by the sex traffickers Lucien is targeting. And if they've brought her to New Orleans rather than sending her immediately to some other destination.

And if they're using a generous timeline rather than one that rushes their cargo immediately to other ports.

I shiver at the word 'cargo'–no human should be called that– and lengthen my strides, the files burning in my arms and the thumb drive nearly humming in my pocket. The moment Lucien gave me access to his network, I jumped onto the computer he loaned me and started downloading everything I could find. An automated search nailed down the files on the girls, and another gave me most of the research Lucien and his team have done. I printed as much as I could in the short time I gave myself, combined it with the file Lucien gave me on the plane, and headed for the door, my phone in my hand.

I don't have my laptop with me–that's still in the beat-up apartment in Brooklyn–but I know someone who'll bring me one. And I want to go through this information in a house that doesn't hold Lucien Boudreaux and his double meanings.

The insinuations.

The annoying new habit of running his fingers over my lips while bending over to breathe me in like I'm some sort of fucking perfume.

I shudder again at that thought, and then at the memory of his lips brushing over my skin, and my body grows hot as the ghost of his touch travels over my neck again. The chill moves up the column of my throat to the spot right behind my ear, then up into my hair, where it disappears, leaving an echo of Lucien on my skin.

Suddenly I want to go back to my suite and take another shower. Wash my hair and get rid of the ghost of his touch.

Because I can't escape the feeling that every time he touches me, he's somehow branding me. Putting a mark on me to tell everyone that I belong to him.

Which is stupid. I don't belong to anyone. Lucien might have owned a piece of me once, but that was a long time ago, and that's where it's going to stay. I don't believe in letting people keep me. My mother gave my father that chance, and look how it turned out. She had to run in the middle of the night to get away from his abuse and divorce him once she was safely in New York, so he didn't blackmail her into staying.

I saw what it did to her, and I'm never going to make that sort of mistake. I don't have time to let Lucien get under my skin again, and I sure as hell don't have time to stand around trading barbs full of double entendre with him. No matter how much his presence feels like the electric filament I've been searching for my entire life.

He let me leave, I remind myself firmly. If he felt any of that electricity, he would have come to New York and searched for me after I ran from New Orleans.

The thought clears the emotion from my heart like it's nothing more than mist, and I walk into the garden with my focus back on my mission. If Aislyn is here and has three days left, that means I have three days to find her and get her out of whatever jam she's in. To do that, I have to know a lot more than I currently do.

Gods, I hope there's something good in the files I stole from Lucien.

I type out a quick text to my chosen partner in crime for the day, stifling a smile when her response comes back, and then head for the garage. Lucien gave in to me with relatively good grace, but put restrictions on my actions, saying I'm allowed access to anything in his house but am not to leave the grounds.

We'll just see about that.

The garages come up suddenly on the other side of the drive-way, and I slow a bit, my eyes roaming over the cavernous building. I count four cars in there–all of them black, of course, and built for speed–but put those to the side. Cars are Sloane's thing. I've always considered them too big, too bulky, and too obvious. I like to make a splash when the situation calls for it, but when you're trying to escape your ex-boyfriend's house without his permission, you need something a little more...

"Ah," I breathe, my eyes finally landing on the smooth black curves of a street bike. I turn for it, my skin buzzing with antici-pation, but come up short when someone steps in my path. I look up, eyes narrowed against the sun and cursing Lucien's men. Who the fuck saw me out here and decided to get in my way, and does he know I'm not supposed to be leaving?

"Where are you going, little lady? Surely you're not heading for those cars when Lucien's specifically said you're not supposed to leave the house."

Well, that answers that question. The men do know, and this one evidently decided to do something about it. I glance at his face, trying to figure out whether I know him, and realize that I do. I actually know him quite well.

"Well Luke Boudreaux," I purr, placing a light hand on his chest and looking up through my lashes. "The last time I saw you, you were what, sixteen? You've grown up." I let my eyes run down his body and back up, doing my best impression of a woman who likes what she sees. It's not hard. Lucien's younger cousin was skinny and gangly when I knew him, but he's gained muscle and height since then. He's got to be taller than Lucien, and that's saying something. He also got his mother's movie star good looks, his hair tousled and blond and his eyes ice blue. His features are so classically handsome that I do almost catch my breath.

On any other day, I would be fluttering my lashes and finding out whether he has a girlfriend–or plans for the night.

As it is, however, I'm pressed for time. And I want to get off this property before Lucien appears out of thin air. The man has a talent for doing just that, and I'd rather not take my chances.

Luke's eyelids flutter as he looks down at my hand, though, and I let my fingers curl so my nails are scratching him a bit.

"You've grown up, too," he said hoarsely. "It's been a long time, Brooks."

"Too long," I murmur. "I didn't realize you were working with Lucien. Moving up in the family? Got your sights on the leadership suite?"

He blushes prettily at that, his fair skin flushing at the implication that he might take over the family, and I run through what I know of the kid, wondering if he's actually making a play. He was so unformed when I knew him, though, that I can't hazard a guess. Still, he's on Lucien's property, and that means Lucien has chosen to bring him into his inner circle.

Given Lucien's trust issues, that says a lot.

"Nothing like that," he stutters. "Just working for Lucien."

"Don't be so humble," I say quickly. I lean forward and drop my voice. "You and I both know that if he brought you to his personal home, it means he trusts you."

Suddenly Luke grins, and I see that he's not as gullible as he would have had me believe. There's craftiness in that smile. A sly understanding of who and what he is, and what he's worth to the family. I grin back, charmed.

"There's the Boudreaux in you," I whisper.

He might not look like Lucien or Gemini, but he's got the craftiness the family is known for, and I put that in my mental notes in case I ever need it.

"What can I say?" he asks. "My mom taught me well."

I tiptoe my fingers up his chest and run one along his jawline. "As she should."

He blushes again and I nearly chuckle. He might be working for Lucien, but he's still young and vulnerable to a pretty woman. Which plays right into my plans.

"Lucien told me to make sure you don't leave," he says suddenly, taking a step back. "Why are you out here?"

Ah. Show time. I shrug like what Lucien said means nothing to me. "He might have told you that, but what he told me is that I can go visit my family while I'm here. He said to borrow any car I want. Or bike." I turn big eyes up to him, forcing myself to look as innocent as possible. "He didn't tell you that?"

Luke shakes his head quickly. "Nope."

"Typical," I snort. "Why don't you go ask him for me? Remind him that I specifically want to see my brother, and he specifically promised that I could. And tell him I'll never forgive him if he thinks he can keep me prisoner here when I want to see my family."

Luke opens his mouth and closes it once, obviously torn.

"You don't want to get in trouble, do you?" I ask quickly. "If you don't let me go when he said I could, he'll be furious."

That does it, and Luke nods and mumbles something about there being nothing wrong with checking. Then he takes off for the house... and I sprint for the Ducati I've already spotted, praying that the keys are in the ignition or close to the bike.

Because I don't think I have time to hot wire the thing right now.

***

I dump the files on the couch in the apartment, drop the thumb drive on top of them, and throw myself into my cousin's arms, laughing.

"It's been too long," I say, grinning so hard my cheeks hurt.

Camille chuckles into my ear, her long blond hair tickling my cheek. "I saw you last week, you goon."

This makes me laugh even harder–partially because hearing her insult anyone in that drawl of hers will never get old–and I draw back. "Seeing you for an hour when we're being held hostage in the catacombs hardly counts."

She raises a perfectly manicured eyebrow and shrugs. "Seems perfectly on brand for time spent with you, honestly. Now what are we doing? Tell me everything."

Typical Camille. I learned a long time ago that the girl was no good in any active situation. Get her into a chase or a gunfight and she'll immediately freeze, leaving you to do all the work for yourself–and save her in the process. I tried to get her to help me figure out what was happening to the girls in the basement, once, and it was such a fiasco that I never asked for her help in that way again. The girl is no Sloane Brennan. Hell, these days she isn't even a match for Penny Lane or Dante Rossi.

But when it comes to research, she's the sharpest tool I have. She can dive into a stack of files and have them organized and memorized in half an hour.

And that's the talent I need right now.

I turn and fan the files out on the couch, then pick up the thumb drive and lift a brow in her direction.

Camille looks from the files to the thumb drive and back, and then grins. "I'll take the files. The laptop is on the dining room table."

And that's all it takes. Camille and I head for our relative workstations–conveniently close, thanks to the fact that the apartment is relatively small–and get to work. I find a bowl of beignets on the table and lift one to my lips, inhaling the smell of fried dough, and catch Camille's eye just before I bite into it.

The first bite is an explosion of sweetness in my mouth, and I moan in ecstasy. "God, I've missed these. No one in New York makes them right."

Camille chuckles. "That's because those heathens insist on boiling their dough rather than frying it. I don't know how you eat anything in that God-forsaken city." She's silent for a beat, and when she looks at me again, her eyes are serious. "I don't know why you stay there at all."

I share a long look with her, thoughts flying through my head as I try to decide what to tell her. Camille is my oldest friend–even older than Sloane, who I've known since I was six and my mother started taking me to New York to spend time with her family–and she knows everything about my life.

Or rather, she knows everything about my life down here. Which means she knew Brooks Landry, the girl I was up until I turned eighteen and deserted New Orleans. Camille knows why I left. She's the only one I told. Her mother, my father's sister, died when she was young, and she moved into my father's house, so we grew up nearly sisters. Her room was right next to mine and I'd run to it any time I needed anything. When I first saw the girls in the basement, I ended up in Camille's bed, whispering to her about what I'd seen.

When my father started beating me, her room was where I hid from him.

And when I learned what my father had in store for me, and that he planned to use me as a spy in the Boudreaux operation, I'd gone to her with my heart in my hands to ask for her help. I was madly in love with Lucien by that time and couldn't stand the thought of leaving him, but also thought he had to be involved in my father's scheme in some way. I'd spent too many years on the rough side of my father's temper and didn't trust any man, and as much as I hated it, that had included Lucien.

Camille had tried to get me to stay. She'd said that Lucien couldn't know what was going on, and pointed out all the reasons that was true. She'd told me to go to him and ask him for help, and that it would be okay. And a part of me had agreed with her.

The bigger part, though–the part that didn't want to let another man take advantage of me and was finished being a pawn for my father–didn't have the patience to wait. That was the part that decided to run for New York in the middle of the night without saying goodbye to anyone.

And Camille doesn't know who I became once I hit the streets of the Big Apple. She doesn't know the girl who has a million and one contacts and can get you anything you need, or the girl who kills without thinking twice if it means she can protect her friends.

Though I doubt she'd be surprised about any of that.

"I stayed there because I built a life I like with people I love," I say simply. "And I didn't want to come home and deal with a man trying to control me."

She nods once, looking thoughtful, and then her lips quirk. "And yet now that you're back, you're supposed to be a prisoner in Lucien Boudreaux' house."

I pop the rest of the beignet in my mouth and grin through the powdered sugar. "And you can see how well that's going for him. Let's get to work."

***

An hour later I'm staring through the window at the colorful balcony across the street from us, trying to give my brain space to put the pieces together. Outside, I can hear a brass band playing and the laughter of tourists, and I shake my head. This apartment was never meant to be quiet enough for thinking. Camille and I bought it when we were sixteen, and have never told anyone it exists. This is where we came when we wanted to get away from my father.

Or to eat beignets.

Or have our fortunes read in the voodoo shop downstairs.

It's tiny and cozy, and we've spent too many nights here, huddling under the covers in the single bed and whispering about the lives we wanted to live one day. I never would have thought, then, that we'd be sitting here now, trying to break through a world of information to uncover a sex trafficking ring.

Though I guess I shouldn't be surprised. New Orleans doesn't function like New York. There's no organization down here when it comes to the underworld. Each family has a rough set of industries they run, and everyone mostly stays in their own lane, but that's not always true. Families and even individuals branch off into new territories without informing anyone else, and there's almost never any cooperation between families.

Records are nonexistent and the truth always depends on who you're talking to.

Even worse, I've been gone for so long that I no longer know who does what. I don't know the girls we're looking at, or which families they belong to. Where they hung out or who they were about to marry.

Camille, on the other hand, knows everything. She's a wealth of information.

"Tell me what Adelaide said again," I say, turning back into the apartment.

Camille looks up, her brow creased. She's been organizing the files into groups of loosely associated girls, and trying to identify where each group spent the most time, in the hopes that it will give us... something.

"She says her father has been keeping more secrets than usual," she says quickly. "He's been raising her to help lead the family and has given her access to most of his records. But he's hiding things lately, and she doesn't know what. Something to do with the entertainment end of his business."

I sit back, chewing my lip. I don't know Addie Lafayette, but I know her father. Etienne Lafayette–or the Crow–has the biggest gambling dens and dance halls in the city. Those dance halls overlap with my father's clubs, which has made them enemies. I don't know how Camille met Addie, but something about their friendship rubs me the wrong way. The Lafayettes aren't friends to the Landry family, and it's odd to me that she's fallen in with them.

But I'm brave enough to admit that it's more than just that.

I don't like that Camille has been here, growing up without me. She has new friends that I don't know, and a boyfriend I've never met. She knows everything about what's going on down here, whereas I'm in the dark.

I hate being in the dark.

I hate even more feeling like I've been left behind.

Which is rich, when I'm the one who did the leaving.

"Think she can push him for information?" I ask. "What could he possibly know? Is it related to all of this?"

Camille's eyes drop to the papers in front of her. "Yes. If these girls are truly disappearing into a sex ring like Lucien thinks, that could border on the dance halls."

I frown. "But would they keep the girls here? Kidnap them here and keep them here?"

"Yes. If they want to make sure the families see who has their girls. If this is a power play, not just a business deal."

A power play.

A business deal.

"If the Crow is involved courtesy of the dance halls," I conclude, "he might not be the only one."

Camille doesn't say anything, and she doesn't have to. I know she's thinking the same thing I am. The Lafayette dance halls are the biggest in the city, so if there's a trafficking ring that's sending girls into entertainment, it makes sense that he'd be the biggest customer.

But there are other dance halls in New Orleans.

Owned by my father.

Which dovetails with what I've already been thinking: that my father is involved in this.

I drop my gaze back to the screen in front of me, trying to distract myself from that thought, but pause, frowning. The laptop has shuffled through the pictures and is now presenting one I haven't seen before. The note attached to it says it's where Lucien suspects one of the girls disappeared. At the very least, it's the last place where she was seen by anyone else.

And I recognize the spot.

I also recognize the logo on the wall.

Because it belongs to my father's organization.

Camille, of course, notices when I gasp. "What?" she asks sharply.

I stare at the screen, wanting to be sure of what I'm seeing, but I know I'm not mistaken. And I know what it means.

"I think this girl disappeared when she was on a Landry property," I finally say.

And though I already suspected that this is where I'd end up, saying it out loud makes it worlds more complicated.

8

LUCIEN

I'm going to kill the man.

And not nicely. It's going to be messy. Bloody. And incredibly dramatic.

"You're not even fucking listening to me," I growl.

"And you don't have any respect, boy," my father snaps back. "You take off for New York at the drop of a hat without giving me any reason. Then you come home with that girl in tow and go right back to your house like you don't have any responsibilities. Do I need to remind you that we have a fucking family to run?"

I clench my hands into fists, ready to punch something. "Of course you don't. I know my job."

"And yet you're still not doing it. If you want to take over, Lucien, you have to play the game. You know what you have to do. Either you get it done, or you're out."

He hangs up before I can answer, and a part of me is glad.

Because that conversation wasn't going to end well, no matter how long we stayed on the phone.

I slam my phone down on the table in front of me and glare at the wall, trying to get my emotions under control. I almost never lose my handle on my temper—I'm famous for it—but talking to my father is uniquely frustrating. The man never saw a guy he didn't want to fight with, and for some reason, I'm his favorite partner when it comes to confrontation. It's always been that way. My mother died when I was ten, courtesy of a rival family's bullet, and the day we buried her, my dad started in on me. He must have thought he was building character or something.

For me, it just felt like he'd decided he hated me as soon as my mom was gone.

Devils, maybe he hated me when she was alive, too, and my mother had just protected me from it. That makes more sense than I like. She was an angel on earth, all blond hair and blue eyes, sparkling laughter and a heart too good for this world. When she died, my world went dark, like the sun disappeared or all the light bulbs had been snuffed out. I'd never thought I was a mama's boy, but life without her was the worst thing I ever experienced. Even worse when my father started treating me like his biggest rival.

I wondered for a long time whether he actually blamed me for her death. I didn't know how he could have, when it was his enemies that killed her. I hadn't even been there. But the ties between my father and I broke the day she left us, and we never managed to rebuild them.

These days, he's trying to threaten my future in the family.

Tomorrow it will be something else.

Even if I give him what he wants—which is what he called about—it won't be enough. He'll just find something else to demand. Some other way to prove that I don't live up to his expectations.

And I never will, as long as he refuses to see what I'm doing. The truth is, he has no idea how seriously I take the family business, mostly because I don't bother to tell him. Why would I? How could I explain what's going on right now? The girls disappearing are bad for business. No, we don't trade in girls, obviously, but we do count on the city to run the way it should, and instead, girls are being snatched off the street.

Our girls. Our sisters and cousins and girlfriends.

And eventually, the kidnappings will bring the feds down on us. New Orleans already walks a fine line between heaven and hell, with an underworld that puts New York to shame. We've got gamblers and hustlers and smugglers, not to mention the dance halls and meat markets. All of it unregulated, and not controlled by anything like New York's Cosa Nostra. No one has control down here, and we like it that way.

The last thing we need is the FBI in our town poking around. But kidnappings draw the wrong sort of attention, and it's only a matter of time before they catch wind of it.

Then there's the deal I made with Brooks.

And the deal I made separately with my father, which I haven't told anyone about yet. Not even Brooks.

I push all thoughts of my father to the side, frustrated that he's managed to get under my skin again, and turn back to my work. Daniel and I are in my office, going through the security footage my contacts have sent me. Looking for the girls we have in our files.

For the moment they disappeared, and who might have taken them.

"What do you have for me?" I ask sharply, counting on Daniel to know what I'm talking about and what I need.

He glances away from the laptop he's been working on, then spins it toward me and comes to stand behind me. One finger on the mouse and two clicks, and we're watching a video. It's grainy and black and white, obviously not from any high-quality camera, but I can see the people clearly.

I can see the girl walking through the parking lot.

"Gods, she's young," I breathe.

"Polly Swift," Daniel agrees. "Related to Crow Lafayette,

though it's not a close relation. Blond, with green eyes. Very pretty. Young."

"How old?" I whisper, hating that I have to know the answer.

"Seventeen."

Satan alive. She's not even allowed to vote yet, and nowhere near close enough to drink alcohol. Though I'm sure she's done the latter. New Orleans starts them young. Still. Only seventeen. She has the rest of her life ahead of her, and instead...

If my suspicions are right, she's been kidnapped by a trafficking ring, and there's only one reason a girl like that gets kidnapped. Well, two: One, for blackmail or money, and since there haven't been any demands for ransom, that we can find, it's not that.

The other answer: sex slavery. Girls and boys taken from their homes and shoved into a world where they're auctioned off to the highest bidder or kept in a harem, forced to serve whoever pays enough for an hour. Slavery. Degradation. Humiliation. The worst betrayal one human can impose on another.

It's disgusting and horrifying and words I don't even have, and I try very hard not to think too much about it. I live on the dark side of the world, my days taken up with gambling, plotting, and murder, but the idea of trading in flesh chills me to my very bones. It's so depraved I can hardly hold it in my head.

Every instinct in my body is screaming to save the girls who have been caught, starting with Brooks' friend. Aislyn Brennan. We don't have any tape on her yet, partially because she was taken in a city where I don't have any contacts, but we're searching.

We just don't have much time.

If we can use some of this footage to identify who's taking them, though, it might lead us to where they're being held. And we might be able to stop them.

"I can't believe we can't get anything better than this," I

growl, leaning closer to the monitor. I'm used to being able to pull the best possible information. My contacts are airtight, and I've never had so much trouble getting information.

But this ring is bigger and sloppier than anything I've ever dealt with. I don't even know if anyone specific is in charge, or if it's just a loose coalition of individuals. It must be organized, to have this much consistency in terms of the victims, but I'll be damned if I can figure out who's at the head of it.

Suddenly Daniel's finger jabs the screen in front of us, and he pauses the video.

"There," he says, pointing.

I look, wondering what he's seeing, and it takes a moment for it to register. The girl is still in the parking lot, but she's walking toward a van, now, as if someone in that van is calling her. Or she knows the person driving it. This is the last-known location for this girl, so we suspect she was kidnapped from this spot. We don't have it on camera. But this is where they got her.

And the van she's walking toward has a logo I know on it.

"Under the City," I say quickly.

"We should have known," Daniel mutters, shoving away from the table and gathering up his things.

I stand and follow him, gathering my guns, knives, and cane just as quickly. Yes, we should have known. Under the City is a bar that sits in the catacombs nears the ocean. It's a swanky place, full of high-end drinks and people with too much money, and it's always rubbed me the wrong way. First of all, they have a gambling den, and gambling is a Boudreaux racket in this town.

Second, they've built the place in the catacombs. Also our territory. We've never been able to kick them out because we don't technically *own* the catacombs, but we've controlled them since the Civil War, when our family took them as part of a smuggling operation.

No, we don't smuggle.

Yes, at that time we used the tunnels to get slaves out of the area and to freedom before they could be sold.

So I lied. Sue me.

If there's a ring smuggling people again, it makes sense that it's happening out of Under the City. It's a where all the wrong people go to gamble and drink. They have access to the ocean and a small pier right outside their door.

Most importantly, the joint is owned by fucking Dominick Landry.

***

I forgot how cold the catacombs are this close to the ocean.

They're always dark and damp, of course, even when you're in the brightest sections. Old beyond measure, their walls have seen far too much. In theory, the tunnels and levees down here were built for flood control, to keep a city caught between the Atlantic and the Mississippi from flooding. New Orleans, you see, shouldn't exist. This is swampland, and sits below ocean level in most places. It was a bad idea from the start, as far as construction went.

But the location, sitting at the mouth of the Mississippi and next to Lake Pontchartrain, and right up against the Gulf of Mexico, meant that whoever controlled this land controlled all shipping in the area. They dictated what came in and out, be it people or goods, and could charge whatever they wanted for the right to use the port.

And money, it turns out, trumps everything. Including whether a city should or shouldn't be placed on land that can hardly hold it because it floods so often.

The Big Easy is therefore full of canals, levees, and underground tunnels that flood when the tides are high, and that should have been the end of it.

It wasn't. Because men like me realized that the tunnels, when not flooded, meant an easy way to get around without anyone else seeing you. Then they realized that you could also smuggle things underground, rather than taking the risk of keeping them on the surface. And the rest, as they say, was history. These walls have seen everything from tobacco to cotton to the men and women they brought in to pick the cotton, and I'm sure they've seen things I haven't even imagined.

Right now, I hope they'll give up some of their secrets.

Like what's happening to girls in Under the City.

I press my back to the wall behind me, snarling as the dampness of the rock seeps into my jacket, and motion toward Daniel. He brought a few men with him, but not many. We aren't on official Boudreaux business, and are in the midst of infiltrating a Landry hot spot. I might be the most important Boudreaux other than my father, but I still don't want to be caught here. Dom Landry and my father have been enemies since they were kids, and Dom's hatred of the Boudreaux extends to me. It eased up when I was set to marry Brooks, but Dom blamed me for her sudden exit from New Orleans, and I've never bothered to try to mend the relationship.

After all, I have plans to take him down one day. Why be friends with someone you intend to destroy?

"What's the plan, boss?" Daniel breathes into my ear.

I consider the question for only a moment. We know a girl disappeared in a parking lot that held a truck labeled as belonging to Under the City. We know Dom Landry owns and runs the club, and I've heard rumors about the kind of clientele he invites here. But that's it.

Part of me wants to rush into the club, guns firing and sword swinging, and demand to be shown the merchandise.

The bigger part of me prefers a more subtle route. Because unlike Dominick, I like to operate in the shadows.

It makes it easier to hide what you're doing.

"We get to the club, find someone, and question them."

Daniel is silent for a beat. "That's it? Find someone and question them?"

I turn, grab his shirt, and push him against the wall. "Do you have a better idea, Daniel? Because I'm getting awfully tired of being told no one has information for me, and I'm doing my best with what little we have."

His eyes shutter and he shakes his head quickly. "If I had a better idea, you'd already know it."

"That's what I thought."

I drop his shirt and spin away from him, my eyes on the door to the club. "It's the middle of the day and the club is closed. We're not going to find bartenders or waitresses in there. If someone is here, they're doing something other than running the club. And if our suspicions are correct, that will mean they have information for us. And we'll do whatever it takes to get that information."

No one answers me, but I assume they understand what that means.

Ten seconds later, I surge toward the door, my eyes racing through the space and my hand on my sword.

***

I slam the man back against the rough stone again, taking too much pleasure in the way his head sounds against the rock.

"Tell me what you're doing here, Simon," I growl. "Because the last time I checked, you didn't exactly do entertainment. You're not here to tend the bar or perform on stage. That's not your bag."

The man in front of me moans in pain and sags a bit, but I pull him up and force him to face me. We found him quickly, thank God, and I recognized him immediately. I've known

Simon leBanc for a long time. We ran scams together when we were kids, though we parted ways when I realized that he was from the wrong side of the tracks for what I had planned in life. These days, he deals with shadier families than mine, doing deals that no decent man would consider.

Like drugs. Hired murders.

Girls.

He's exactly the kind of man I'd expect to find tangled up in a trafficking ring, and the moment I saw him, I knew we had our quarry. Now we just need to get him to talk.

"I don't know anything," he says again. "Come on, man. You and me, we go way back."

"Which means I know exactly what sort of person you are," I answer casually. "Daniel, his fingers."

"No!" Simon screams, but he has no say in the matter. Not really.

Before he can say anything else, Daniel's picked up one of his hands, put it against the stone, and brought the butt of his gun down on the man's forefinger, shattering it.

Simon screams and sags again, and I pin him harder to the wall.

"Tell me what you're doing here, Simon," I repeat. "Or you're going to lose more than your fingers."

"And you're going to lose more than that if you keep poking around," he snarls. "This is bigger than you, Boudreaux. Bigger than us both."

I motion to Daniel and he singles out another finger.

"No!" Simon screeches. "I'm telling you everything I know. This is big. Bigger than any New Orleans family. And they'll take you down without thinking twice. Kill me if they even know I've spoken to you." He turns his head and meets my gaze, his eyes bloodshot and terrified. "Stay out of this, or we'll both lose our lives."

Suddenly I hear movement down the tunnel from us and

freeze, my mind skipping through the possibilities. It's too early for the club to be opening, which means whoever that is might be smugglers. Probably armed. I only have four men and we're not heavily armed. We're not here on official Boudreaux business.

I'm not willing to get caught before I'm ready.

I lean toward Simon, furious at being interrupted. "I want to know what's going on here, and I'll rip the city apart to find out. Once I do, I'll kill everyone involved. You tell that to your boss. See how he feels about having made an enemy of the biggest family in New Orleans."

We turn and leave before the footsteps reach us, without anything but a possible location, and the knowledge that whoever is running this ring, they're not hiring the best people. Simon leBanc is a mercenary. An outlaw. And if they're using him, it's because no honorable family will work with them.

This just got a whole lot more complicated. And I don't like complications.

9

BROOKS

I get to my father's mansion without a real plan for what I'm going to do, and that's so unlike me that I have to pause before I hit the driveway and get my brain to actually think.

The moment I saw that logo in the photo at the apartment, I knew what it meant. Honestly, I've had the thought since Aislyn first went missing, and then again when Lucien told me girls were disappearing, and then again when I saw all those files. Even if I hadn't thought about it consciously, my subconscious was making sure I remembered the girls filing through the hall in the basement, years ago. I've been dreaming about it since the war with the Poffo clan, though the two don't seem to have anything to do with each other.

Something inside me knew this was going to happen. When I saw my father's mark on that building, the pieces just fell into place.

And you'd think that would mean I know what the fuck I'm going to do about it. But you'd be wrong. Because for possibly the first time in my life, I don't have a plan ready-made for this.

Maybe because 'this' is a situation where I suspect my father is buying and selling girls for sex and money, and doing it despite how deranged and disgusting it is.

I snort at that. 'Deranged and Disgusting' could be my father's middle name. Names.

I sit on the bike and stare up at the gates of the mansion, with their wrought iron curves and embellishments, and let my mind travel beyond them to the house. It's huge and gothic, gray stone with turrets and a ridiculous roof, and the inside is just as bad. My father is sleek and modern, but his house is gaudy and overdone, like he went to the kingdom of the Sun King to get the internal decorations. Everything is done in gold and burgundy, with plush carpets and dark wood. And you'd think, with all that gold, that the place would shine like the sun, but the opposite is true.

The house is cold and dark and very intense. It reeks of evil. Particularly at night.

A shiver passes over my skin and I move on from the house, trying to gather what I know. I suspect that my dad is buying and selling girls, or at least moving them for someone else, and given what I've seen before, this isn't a reach. If he was doing it when I was a kid, and making money, I don't see any reason he'd stop. But according to our research, the game has changed. The girls I saw when I was thirteen were scratched up and dirty. Street girls who didn't have anyone to save them. The girls I've seen in the files from Lucien are from a higher class. Girls with money and guards. Families who should have protected them.

Those aren't the sorts of girls you traffic because it's easy, and I want to know what the fuck my father's playing at.

I also want to know who's paying him to do it–or who's buying them from him. I've seen enough in New York to know that no one works alone in a racket like this, even in New Orleans, where everyone is a freelancer. There are hundreds of girls in those files, which means this is a big ring. Too big for him to run on his own.

If I can figure out who's pulling my dad's strings, I might be able to stop all of this.

And if my timeline is correct, I only have a couple days to do it before Aislyn is shipped off to wherever they've promised someone a girl.

Right. That means I don't have time to be sitting out here playing the guessing game. I leave the bike where it is and walk to the gates, pushing them open like I still own the place. I know how I look as I'm walking up the driveway: like I know exactly what I'm doing, and like I don't have a doubt in the world.

It's not true. But no one else needs to know that. The only thing they need to know is that I'm back, and I want back in. Actually, I only need one person to think that.

My father.

Because if I can go in there and convince him that I'm on his side–that I'm home and want to come back into the family–I might be able to get information the easy way. And that will mean getting to Aislyn more quickly.

I can do it, I assure myself. I can act like his friend for an hour. Maybe two. Especially if it means getting what I want.

And then afterward, I'll do the other thing I came down here for.

Mission 1: Save the girls.

Mission 2: Take my father down, and bury him in a grave no one will ever fucking find.

***

He's waiting for me at the top of the steps that lead up to the front door, a smirk on his mouth and his shirt unbuttoned at the top, like he was just sitting down for dinner. All casual and relaxed, his hands hanging open at his sides and his stance easy.

All a lie.

But I force my shoulders down and a smile onto my face, to match his attitude. I even make that smile as friendly as possible. I can do this. I can play nice. For a little.

"Dad," I say, reaching for bashful and charming.

"Daughter." The word is friendly but cautious, as if he's not sure he can believe what his eyes are telling him right now.

Smart.

"Did you walk here? Because I would have sent a car for you."

It takes me no time flat to see that statement for what it is. Bait. He wants to know why I'm in town and whether I'm here with anyone else. Where I'm staying. Whose side I'm on.

"I've got a bike at the front gate," I say, stepping up the stairs and coming to a stop facing him. "But I wanted a walk before I saw you."

His face grows even more cautious. "Why?"

Time to lie, Brooks.

"Because the last time I saw you it didn't go well, and I wanted to make sure this time was better." I say it without my voice cracking, which is a feat of strength unto itself, and without rolling my eyes at the lie.

Also a miracle.

He considers that for a moment, staring into my eyes and waiting for me to break, and I hold eye contact and tip my chin up, daring him to question my motives. I can tell from the look on his face that he doesn't know how long I've been in town or why I'm here. If he did, he'd already be so angry he wouldn't speak to me.

Thank you, Lucien, I think, glad for the first time that he's able to move through the city like smoke, leaving very little evidence behind him. Evidently when I'm with him, I'm hidden in that smoke, and that almost makes being around him worthwhile.

Almost.

"Dinner?" he suddenly asks. "I was just sitting down for steak."

I almost laugh. That was a whole lot easier than I expected it to be. The fact that he didn't take one look at me and kick me out is a miracle. After all, the last time we were here I told him I was going to kill him.

To be fair, he'd just refused to give me men to save my friends, so I had a good reason. It was why I went to Lucien in the first place–though 'going' to Lucien wasn't exactly how it happened. I'd been on my way there, sure, but I was kidnapped first, by Lucien's second-in-command and at Lucien's bidding. Camille and I found ourselves in the catacombs, trapped with a group of Boudreaux men, when a group of Landry men attacked us.

I never found out why they attacked, and suddenly I'm not so sure of my father's welcome. The men who came after us in the catacombs worked for my father, and if Lucien and his men hadn't protected us, Camille and I would both be dead right now.

Or, if my suspicions about him are correct, worse.

I fight to keep from narrowing my eyes at the memory. He can't know that I suspect anything. I'm here for information, not to blow my cover. I learned a long time ago that sometimes a girl needs to keep her brain to herself, and that usually means withholding more information than you give up.

Men tend to underestimate how much a girl can do.

And that always leads to an advantage for the girl.

So I give him my sweetest, most innocent smile–one of the biggest lies I've ever told in my life–and tell him I'd love to have dinner, and steak sounds terrific. Then I follow him into the house, already planning how I can ditch him and get into his office without him knowing about it.

***

The house is exactly how I remember it–not shocking, since I saw it just a week ago–but I fight the need to turn around and run back out again. This place doesn't hold many happy memories for me. My father screaming at my mother. Me and my brother hiding in each other's rooms when the dark became too dense at night, the sounds of the house too frightening.

All the girls I couldn't save.

The things my father did to me when I tried.

This was where it all started, my need for control and the knowledge that no one was going to come for me when I needed help. I spent too much time comforting my mother after he hit her, and even more time running to my brother and begging him to tell me it would be okay. And I learned early on that no one else could make it okay for me. My brother couldn't make the dark any less scary, and my mother couldn't make my father stop hitting me. No one could help me save the girls in the basement, and I'd been too young and small to do it myself.

Being here in this new guise, with my guns and knives and all the street smarts I gained in New York, is like seeing the place with different eyes. I'm not here to ask my father for anything, and that frees me, as well. I'm here to take information, by hook or by crook, and that right there?

That's pretty fucking empowering.

We sit at the enormous table in the dining room, despite the fact that there are only two of us, and I fight to make small talk with my father while we work our way through some of the most delicious steak I've ever had. To my surprise, he's willing to talk business with me, going through some of his biggest shipments to date and saying that he has some new business ventures on the rise. He's grooming my brother, Beau, to take over, and that's taking up most of his time. No, he's not thinking about getting remarried, though he is shopping for a wife for Beau.

I don't want to hear about that, though. I go back to the new business ventures.

"Brand new?" I ask. "Or just ventures that you're expanding to be bigger?"

The shock passes through his eyes so quickly that I almost miss it, and then it's replaced by a sly, crafty look that closes his face off to me.

"Brand new," he says. "Things I've never tried before but want to get into."

Liar.

"What sorts of things?" I ask, taking a drink of my wine. How far will he go with this lie? Does he have a cover story already made up, in case someone asks?

But evidently we've reached the end of sharing time, because he brings a hand down sharply on the table. "That, my dear, is none of your concern. You left the family, in case you've forgotten. Which means our business dealings are none of your... well, business."

His mouth quirks at his own joke, and I have to fight to keep myself in my chair. God, I hate the man. I hate his arrogance and condescension and the unreal, overwhelming belief that he's better than anyone else.

I hate that he can sit there looking suave as you please, like nothing is wrong, when he's facing the daughter he very nearly killed with his fists.

And a part of me hates myself for sitting across from him and playing nice, when all I want to do is slit his throat.

But needs must.

I lean onto my elbows and pin him with a stare. "Maybe I want to come back into the family. Come home and take my rightful place."

He tips his head and stares at me like he's trying to see through the lie, and I think for a moment he won't believe me. He still hasn't asked why I'm in town or who I'm here with, and

I'm sure it's eating him up not to know. He's got to realize that I wouldn't just come down here and show up at his door, asking to be let in like some sort of Orphan Annie.

Or maybe he doesn't.

"That sounds like quite a plan," he says, bland and unreadable. "And I'd be happy to have you. Why don't we start with a reintroduction into our world? The family is having a ball tomorrow night. Why don't you join us? I'd like to introduce you to some... people."

I frown. Did I imagine the emphasis on the word 'people'? The pause? The crafty glint of his eye? Is this a trick? A trap?

Even if it is, can I afford to turn it down? Because if he's behind the kidnappings, I need a way into his organization. And a ball where I'm presented to his contacts might be just the ticket.

"That sounds lovely," I reply. "Though if it's a ball..." I let my voice fade away, leaving the implication that I didn't exactly bring a ball gown with me to New Orleans.

Instead of replying, my father snaps his fingers and looks behind me. I turn to see his butler coming in, carrying a large box.

"A welcome home present," my father says smoothly.

I glance at him, confused, then take the box from the butler and open it. Inside, I find a deep green satin ballgown. And when I look at the tag, it's my size.

My heart drops into my stomach and I look up to see that my father is grinning. And it's not a nice grin.

"I'll see you tomorrow night," he says smoothly. "At Under the City. Nine sharp."

He stands and walks out of the room without saying goodbye, and I watch him go, my skin crawling with the knowledge that he did know I was in town. And that he knows what size dress I wear.

And that my favorite color is green.

I give myself a full five minutes to feel off balance about the whole thing, and more than a little terrified. Then I hear him go upstairs to his room, and grin almost as widely as he did.

Moments later, I'm up and hustling toward the office he keeps on the first floor. And the computer he has in there. As long as his passwords haven't changed, I can be in and out in ten minutes, max.

***

It takes me twelve, but it's worth the danger of the extra two minutes.

The idiot has the file sitting in plain sight on his desktop, and it has more information than I could have hoped for. I don't have time to upload it to the cloud so I can look later, but I take as many pictures as I can–names of girls, locations, and time-lines–and then zero in on something he has on his calendar for today. A sight highlighted with a code that I've seen attached to the names of other girls in the file.

That code has to mean a girl is going to be either picked up or dropped off.

And this time and date comes with an address.

I walk as quickly as I can from the house, trying to look both elated about the dress–which is actually beautiful–and like I've just had a lovely dinner with Dear Old Dad.

The truth, of course, is somewhat different. Because he might not have wanted to tell me anything, but that doesn't mean I'm out of the game. I've got an address and a time, and that's really all I need for now.

I'm going hunting. And my dad's operation is the target.

10

LUCIEN

Night has fallen by the time we get back to the mansion, and it's well and truly dark out by the time I'm standing from my research, stretching, and going to stare out the window. Technically we're in the basement, in what I've built as the war room, but really it's half of the first floor of the house.

Because I've always liked the idea of an underground war room. But I live in New Orleans, and this is a town that floods regularly. We don't have the foundation for underground rooms, and if we built them anyhow, they would flood often enough to make them pointless.

This room might as well be underground, though. This is the sole window, the rest of the room made up of stark brick walls and concrete floors. Maps and screens line the room, giving us a 360-degree view of whatever we're researching at the time, and several tables in the middle of the room hold ten different computers. Their screens are all lit up right now, though Daniel and I are the only ones in the room. We have the lights turned low because I think better that way, and have been going through list after list of boats heading in and out of the New

Orleans port. And the train stations. And even the trucking yards.

I believe I know who's buying and selling girls, now. Simon leBanc was at Dom Landry's club, acting suspicious enough that I'm sure he was doing something nefarious, and upon further research, we found that several of the missing girls have disappeared from Landry properties. But that doesn't give me much. I'm not exactly going to go to the Landry mansion, have a steak dinner with Dominick, and demand to know what he's up to.

Even if I did, it wouldn't solve the biggest problem.

We need to know when the next shipment of girls is leaving, so we can stop it before we lose them forever. I would bet my whole fortune that Brooks' friend is in that shipment, and though it doesn't matter to me whether Brooks finds her or not —Brooks' problems are her own—I'm honor-bound to make sure no other girl is sent away from our shores.

I can't *not*. But it doesn't have anything to do with Brooks.

Seriously.

The problem is, the girl Brooks is searching for is very hard to find. We tracked her from New York to Atlanta, and then to New Orleans, but her trail went dead as soon as she arrived here. They must have taken her immediately underground, because no one seems to have seen her since then. I only know she arrived because I found a man who was working at the train station when she came in and recognized the fact that she wasn't from New Orleans.

He was also more than willing to talk, when I paid him enough.

So she arrived in town, and then disappeared.

God, I hope she hasn't been shipped out yet. Brooks is intent on finding her, and I can't imagine how she'll react if we fail.

If she fails. Because this is her problem, not mine.

"Let's go over what we have so far," I say, seeking to distract myself. "We have enough girls missing that it can't be a coincidence. And we know that some are local, but others aren't. This points to one thing: Someone in New Orleans is running girls, and they're stealing them from other cities."

"That just about sums it up," Daniel says from behind me. "Boss, I have something."

The urgency in his voice has me spinning immediately, excited at the thought that he might have found something new. I'm at the table in seconds flat, and leaning over the shipping manifest he's looking at.

"What is it?"

"The manifest for the Destiny," he says quietly. "It comes in and out of port once a month, on a schedule. Always arrives empty. Always leaves full."

Well that's suspicious. Shipping companies make their money by hauling shipments from one port to another. They might arrive carrying food and leave carrying textiles, and pick up additional loads as they go. They never sail empty unless they have to. No load means no money.

"They'd arrive empty so they didn't have to record their arrival," I say quietly. "No registration with the authorities if there's nothing to register."

"Exactly. And she's here now. Just... waiting."

My stomach does an excited flip. "When is she due to leave again?"

Daniel looks up and meets my gaze. "Three days from now."

Three days.

Exactly the timeline we've guessed at for the next load of girls, if we use Aislyn's kidnapping as the starting point. A week to get enough girls to fill a load. Long enough to have plenty of captives, but quick enough to guarantee they don't have to hold the girls for long.

I don't trade in flesh, but even I can see that it isn't the sort of cargo you want to hold for long. Too many things might go wrong. Girls getting sick or dying, other people stealing them, or worst of all, one of them escaping and telling the authorities.

If they're working with a one-week timeline...

Well, it's confirmation we didn't have before.

"How are they listing the cargo they're shipping out?" I ask, morbid curiosity getting the better of me.

"They don't have it specified," Daniel says quietly. "They've listed it as though they don't know what the cargo is, yet. Like they're shopping for a load."

I laugh softly. "And I bet they never correct that. Because without a cargo, they don't have to take the chance of someone coming on board to investigate."

"Or paying taxes on it."

I frown, letting my mind run through the facts. It seems too clean. Too easy. I don't like it. I'm used to problems I have to work to solve, and this doesn't seem right. We just find the ship with a mystery cargo, and get the time and date it's sailing?

Too easy.

There must be a trick in there somewhere, but what could it be? What if it's the wrong ship and we chase it only to find an empty container? What if they're setting us up? What if it's a bait and switch, meant to draw us out into the open so they can slaughter us when we try to save girls and only find a bunch of guns in the ship? Do they even know we're on their tails?

They will if Simon speaks to whoever he works for.

"We need proof," I conclude. "So we can protect ourselves. We need more information."

"More information about what?" a new voice asks.

I jump and turn in the same motion, my hand going to the knife strapped to my chest, though I already know that voice. I just didn't expect it in my house.

This isn't, after all, where she actually lives.

"What in devils are you doing here?" I ask.

Corinne, my little sister and the baby of the family, stands at the door to the room, looking as bratty and entitled as ever, and for a moment my heart warms. She's six years younger than me, so by the time she was born, I was old enough to help, and I've loved her with my entire soul ever since. When my mother died, four years after she was born, I took her under my wing and made sure my father couldn't touch her.

She's the only member of my family I would die for.

Unfortunately, she knows it, and is not opposed to taking advantage of my soft side. She tips her head back and forth, her long brown hair swinging, and I wonder if she practices that motion in the mirror just for the effect.

It would be like her.

"I heard my big brother was acting strangely. Creeping through catacombs in the middle of the night and fighting with men he shouldn't even be associating with. I also—" She turns large, dark eyes to me and lifts a brow. "—Heard you have a friend in town. I figured I better come make sure she hasn't skinned you alive yet."

I grit my teeth, caught between extreme anger at her butting into my affairs, uninvited, and amusement at how freaking good she's gotten at this game. Officially, she's not supposed to be involved in the family business. My father's worked hard to keep her clean, or so he says, and he would be furious if he knew I was dragging her into things.

Except she drags herself, because she refuses to stay out of it. And she's getting good. One of these days, she might even be a match for me in her intelligence gathering.

But right now, she's still a kid, only twenty-two to my twenty-eight, and she does not need to be caught up in an investigation on a trafficking ring that kidnaps and sells girls her age. She's pretty and young and looks innocent, though she's not, and if she's in the wrong place at the wrong time, she'll make herself a target.

"All of that is exactly none of your business, Corinne. And you know it."

"And yet here I am, making it my business." She shrugs in a way that makes her look more French than American, and now I'm annoyed.

"You're here putting your nose into someone else's business, as usual. That doesn't make it okay."

She just grins and starts walking toward me, her eyes already on the computers. "What are you going to do about it? Kick me out?"

I step into her path, grab her shoulders, turn her around, and start pushing her back toward the door. "Yes. We're looking at something that I don't even want you knowing about, much less helping with. And I won't risk you."

I don't tell her what we're doing, because it's none of her business.

And because she's still a kid, innocent and naive—despite what she'd tell you—and doesn't need to know about the seedier things that happen in this city. She definitely doesn't need to see it. And there's a voice in my head screaming that we're lucky she hasn't been caught up in it yet. She's the right age, and beautiful in a way that's made me uncomfortable for years.

She's from the right sort of family.

The Boudreaux haven't lost anyone important yet. Some distant cousins. But that doesn't mean it won't happen. Particularly if she starts making herself obvious to the very men who might steal her.

She jerks out of my hands, though, and dashes around me back to the computers. "That's not your call to make, Lucien, and you know it."

I grab her again, and am in the process of pushing her out when Daniel stops me.

"Boss."

I look at him, my hands on Corinne's shoulders, and see that he's holding up another picture. Two of them.

"Two more girls who disappeared from a Landry property."

Shit.

I drop my sister and head for Daniel, mind spinning. "What do you mean?"

"The last footage of them has them in the same parking lot. The one with the van from Under the City. Footage of them heading for the van, and then nothing. These are them."

He lays the two photos on the table and spreads them enough to let me see. Two girls who could be twins, I think. Both pretty in a generic sort of way, blond and blue-eyed, and very young. Nothing stands out about them except their names.

Both are Masons.

They're not attached to the mafia, then, or not that I know of. Because I know the Mason family. They run the city, but not from the underworld. They're the biggest above-board businessmen in New Orleans, though. Construction, permitting, development, and rentals, to start with. Their girls aren't mafia molls or wives. They're debutantes. Party girls. Society darlings.

They're even less connected to crime, and should never even have contact with the sort of men who would kidnap them and sell them to slavers.

I knew girls like this were involved. Hell, I've told Brooks as much. But there's something about seeing it in full color that makes my stomach turn with even more disgust. I've grown up in this world and have the heart and soul of a pirate. I'll kill men for looking at me the wrong way, and never regret it. And I'll cheat you out of your entire fortune in one of our gambling dens.

But touching girls is so far out of line that not even my brain can wrap around it.

"I know those girls," a voice says immediately to my right. "Why do you have pictures of them?"

I look down to find that Corinne has invited herself right into the conversation—no surprise—and is fingering the pictures, brushing her forefinger over the face of Victoria Mason.

Dammit. I can't think quickly enough to come up with a story for why we'd have pictures of girls sitting in our war room, and end up making a split-second decision for the truth. I don't want to tell her, but she's caught me in a bad moment, and I can't exactly say we're doing research on girls for no reason.

She'd be immediately suspicious.

"We're researching some disappearances," I say, keeping it short. "Too many girls are disappearing, and it's not just New Orleans. New York, Boston, Atlanta..."

She nods once. "That makes sense. You suspect a smuggling ring."

Gods, this girl is sharp. Almost as sharp as me. "We do."

When she turns her eyes up to me, they're just as intelligent as I feared. She already knows what's going on. Maybe she came here knowing, and has just found confirmation for her assumptions. "Is that why Brooks is back in town? Or did she come here just for you?"

"She's not here for me," I snap, angrier than I should be at her insinuation.

Because Brooks should be here for me, and she's not, and I guess I'm just not okay with that.

Corinne shuts her mouth, but her eyes are laughing at me, and I reach down and snatch the pictures out from under her nose.

"Do you have anything to add to this conversation or are you just here to annoy me?"

"That's rich. You were just trying to kick me out and now you want me to help? My, how the tables have turned."

I growl, about ready to kick her back out, but she suddenly decides she's going to play nicely.

"Actually, I do. I know both those girls, to start with, but I also remember when they disappeared. You must. Their families made such a big deal of it. The news did stories, their fathers offered rewards, everyone was searching. And then it just went away. Like the tap had been turned off."

Now that she says it, I do remember. These girls went missing on the same day, and the story was wild. Everyone in town was talking about it because their fathers were brothers, and very rich. And then it just... stopped.

"As if their families had been told to keep it down," I murmur, finishing the thought out loud.

"Forced, probably," Daniel responds. "By someone."

Yes. That... actually makes a surprising amount of sense. The girls being taken are outside of what I'd expect. These are high-level families, with lots of money, but there's evidently no ransom being asked for them. They're not given the chance to buy them back.

So whoever is doing this has plenty of money. They're looking for something else.

Power.

Or revenge.

"Find other patterns," I say sharply. "Girls who are related or disappeared at the same time. And start making a list of the families who've been hit. Figure out what they have in common."

"Like a common enemy?" Daniel asks.

"Exactly."

The three of us get to work immediately, going back through all the files with new eyes and looking for families rather than kidnapping sites or girls. I want to know what connects everyone to each other, because I don't think it's just the fact that they had girls worth stealing.

I think this is a whole lot bigger than just a sex trafficking ring.

Within half an hour, though, I realize that no matter what we find here, it's not going to be enough. We're finding the same families again and again, one way or another, but that doesn't tell us why, and it certainly doesn't tell us who.

"This isn't giving us enough," I say finally. "And it's not going to help us save the girls who ship out next."

"What's the timeline?" Corinne asks, picking up on the game quicker than I would have liked. There is no good reason for my baby sister to understand things like timelines for girls being shipped to other countries as sex slaves.

But I'll deal with making new rules for her later.

"Three days, and that's just the group we know about."

"Based on?" she asks.

"A certain high-level kidnapping from New York," I say. Then, in my own defense: "The one Brooks is investigating."

This gets a sly smile from my sister, a raised eyebrow, and a nod.

"And find some shipping manifests," I demand. "Ones that can actually tell us something."

"Right," she murmurs. She shuffles through the papers for a second, then looks at me again. "But we're not going to find enough here to stop it."

I nod, glad for once that her mind works so quickly. "Exactly. I need..." I think about it for a moment, but the answer is obvious. "I need a man on the inside."

There's a beat of silence, and then Corinne says, "And what are you going to do when Brooks comes to the same conclusion and puts herself in their hands?"

I close my eyes, having already thought of the possibility myself, and knowing exactly what I'll do. "Then I burn New Orleans down to get her out."

This brings up a realization, though, and I look around the room, suddenly concerned. Speaking of Brooks, where the hell is that girl? I've been home for hours now, and I haven't seen hide nor hair of her. I would have expected her to be down here forcing me to include her in the planning.

No, she doesn't know about this room, but details like that have never stopped Brooks Landry.

"Where the fuck *is* Brooks?" I ask, suddenly very nervous. "Have we seen her since we got back? Where's she been all day?"

No one answers, and I'm striding for the door before I can think, my mind on nothing but the red-haired beauty and the fact that she comes up with so-called plans so fast it makes your head spin.

And that they're almost always dangerous or stupid. Or both.

11

BROOKS

I lean down over the Ducati, my stomach to the casing around the tank and my eyes on the road ahead as I shoot through the dark night. It's past full dark now and the city around me is starting to put on its night-time face. Street lamps and lights flash above me as I drive, and I can hear music starting to play from the houses around me. People are on the sidewalks making their way to the clubs and restaurants, if they're looking for legal entertainment, and the dance halls and gambling dens if they're not. Everyone is chatting and laughing as if they don't have a care in the world.

Because they don't know that the world is falling apart around them.

Or maybe that's just me.

I go through what I know again, collecting all the information I managed to store in my brain. Most of the details are on my phone, thanks to the pictures I took, but I can remember a few things. The name of the girl. Anastasia Brayden. The time for the operation: 10PM. The location where they're either picking her up or dropping her off.

For that, I only have an address, and I wonder suddenly what

I'm going to find there. It's near the port, almost on top of the water, though I know that only because Lucien used to take me to that area to get into the catacombs through some secret entrance he thought only he knew about. My mind snags on that and I suddenly remember those days, when we were newly engaged and learning each other in a whole new way. We'd been friends for years–or at least acquaintances who spent as much time together as we could whenever I was in town–and had kissed several times already.

When we found out we were going to be married, courtesy of the contract between our fathers, we'd both been giddy with excitement. We'd run through the city every night like a couple of kids with all the money in the world to spend, and I thought at the time that I would never be happier. I thought I'd found the love of my life, and my partner in crime.

I never thought I'd find out that my father was sending me to the Boudreaux house as a plant, or that I'd come to the conclusion that Lucien had to be in on it.

I also didn't think Lucien would let me go. Which was why I left in the middle of the night without telling anyone but Camille. I thought Lucien would try to stop me, and even after I left, I thought he'd come after me.

News flash: He didn't. He never even called. Didn't write or send carrier pigeons, and when I asked, Camille told me he'd never approached her, asking for my location. Instead, he'd gone right into the city and started dating every girl he could get his hands on.

"Asshole," I breathe.

I bend down further and push the bike to go even faster. I don't have a lot of time between now and whatever's happening at 10. I want to get to the address and find a place to hide before anyone else arrives. This is the best intel I've found so far, and I'm going to make it count.

The plan: Get to the drop-off (or pick-up) point and get my

eyes on the girl in question. Then watch. I want to see who takes her and whether they have any identifying marks. If I can figure out who they're working for, it'll be perfect.

If I can stick with them and see where they take her, even better.

I'll gather as much evidence as I can, and then save the girl and get the fuck out of there before anyone comes to help. That's the easy part, though; I've got plenty of practice taking men down, so saving her will be easy.

As long as I get there in time.

As long as that code I saw on my father's calendar means what I think it means.

I see the turn I need ahead and chance a glance over my shoulder, to make sure no one is going to get in my way. I don't think anyone saw me leave my father's house, so I should be in the clear, but you never know.

When I look back, I see a sedan I've never seen before. It's dark, the windows completely blacked out, and fast. I know it wasn't there five minutes ago because I've been checking the rear-view mirror, just to make sure. It must have come from some other street, and the noise of the New Orleans night is so raucous that I didn't notice it.

Shit.

Well, that doesn't necessarily mean that he's following me. Maybe he just decided to drive to the club rather than walk.

I take aim at the street I want and slow just enough to make the turn, skidding through it at a speed that's barely safe, the tires jumping along the asphalt below me and screeching when I hit the gas again. I shoot up the street, trying to gain as much speed as possible. If that guy is following me, he won't be able to take the corner as quickly. I want to have plenty of distance between us by the time he gets straight again.

When I glance over my shoulder, though, I'm shocked at what I see. He's taken the corner at a speed I wouldn't have thought possible, performing a nearly perfect Tokyo drift to get around it without tipping the car onto its side.

God dammit.

I turn back around and slam on the accelerator, rethinking my route and trying to put as many turns in as I can afford. I don't have a lot of time to get to the destination, but I also don't want to get there with company. I don't know who the fuck is in that car, but if they're taking a corner like that, they're a better driver than anyone I've ever met.

And they're evidently set on catching me.

***

By the time I reach my destination I'm breathing heavily, strung out on adrenaline and stress and feeling jittery.

But I also lost the guy. I'm sure of it. I took corners he couldn't take and used alleys he wouldn't fit in, and he fell behind me ten minutes ago. I've kept a close eye on my mirrors and haven't seen him since, and I think I might have actually pulled it off.

I bring the bike to a stop and wheel it up next to a building, where it's hidden in the shadows. Beyond me, a parking lot sits bright and well-let in the darkness.

And beyond that, a graveyard full of vaults and headstones.

I frown at that, trying to remember which cemetery this is, and remember so suddenly that it feels like my head is going to explode with the knowledge. I've seen that cemetery before. Many times. Lucien used to bring me here as often as he could.

Because that's where his supposedly secret entrance to the catacombs is.

I grab for my phone, panicked that I remembered the address

wrong, and pull up the picture I took of my dad's screen. Then I glance at the building next to me, and then the street sign.

This is the right address. But there's nothing here except a parking lot and a graveyard. What the fuck am I doing here, and how are they going to kidnap a girl from a fucking graveyard?

Before I get any further into that thought a squeal of tires announces someone coming in hot, and I jump back against the wall next to my bike as a car barrels into the parking lot, then comes to hard stop. The engine cuts and there's silence for a full moment.

Long enough for me to recognize the car that was following me.

I slide my hand into my jacket and grab the knife I always wear against my chest, then pull my Glock out of the holster on my back. I didn't expect to use them this early, but I came armed. And this guy is about to find out why following me into a dark parking lot is a bad idea. I'm busy. I don't need company.

When he opens the door and steps out of the car, though, all growling, piratical menace, I realize that it's Lucien.

I sag, the adrenaline rushing out of me like someone's put a drain in my side, and have to stop myself from actually running to him. I've torn though the night–and my father's house–without allowing myself to think about it too much, and at the sight of someone friendly–someone I used to trust with my life–I suddenly realize how much I've needed backup. Suspecting that my father is behind everything, then facing him, then racing toward this parking lot without knowing for sure what I was going to do...

I didn't give myself any time to think about it. But now that I see Lucien I know that a part of me was waiting for him to come support me.

And the moment I realize it, I put it away. Because I might have trusted him once, but that was a long time ago. These days, I don't know who he is or what he wants. I do know that he's keeping secrets from me. And I don't like when people keep secrets.

Though his face when he tears toward me tell me that he dislikes me almost as much as I dislike him right now.

"What are you doing here?" I ask. "And how the hell did you find me?"

Instead of answering, he reaches behind my ear, making me twitch, and pulls something out of my hair, holding it up in front of my face.

"When I realized you were missing and found my idiot cousin to ask what happened, I called Camille, who was kind enough to tell me that you'd gone to your father's house. And then I turned on the tracking device."

I shove him back, even angrier than I was thirty seconds ago. "You put a tracking device on me?"

He grins. "Of course I did."

I didn't think I could get angrier, but I was wrong. I want to slap the grin right off his face. "Why?"

He bites his lip and gets as close to me as he can without actually touching me. "Because I've known you a long time, Brooks. And I know you're almost never where you're supposed to be. I figured I'd need a way to find you before you got into any trouble. Now what the fuck are we doing here?"

I open my mouth to answer but anger and shock have stolen my voice, and it takes me several minutes to remember how to speak. By the time I get there, I've gone through a change of heart. I don't like that he's here and I fucking hate that he had the nerve to put a tracking device on me. I want to slice his throat right here and now for daring.

But a very large part of me is disturbingly glad to see him, and more than a little bit heated at how close he is right now. His woodsy scent is flooding my head and bringing back all sorts of memories, and somewhere inside me a little girl is screaming for someone to take care of her, and chanting Lucien's name again and again and again.

She wants to believe we can still trust him, and that he might be the knight in shining armor we've always wanted.

I know he's not. He's a shadowy, smooth-talking pirate who will always choose what's best for himself.

But as long as he's offering to help, I'm going to let him.

Just to give that little girl a moment of hope.

"I broke into my father's computer in his office and found the files he's keeping on this trafficking ring," I say quickly. "Yes, he's involved. No, I don't know who he's working for. Yes, there were a lot of names and I took pictures. He had a meeting set up on his calendar for this spot, starting in five minutes. And the code indicated that a girl would be either picked up or dropped off. I came to get to one of the men and find out what's going on. And to get the girl the hell out of here."

He blinks once, like he's having trouble taking all of that in, and then scowls. "And you were going to do all of that without me?"

I just shrug. "I figured you were busy."

He gives me a dark, humorless chuckle. "Never too busy for you, love. Let's get set up."

12

LUCIEN

I can't believe she was going to run this mission without me.

I mean, I can. Of course she was. This girl never does anything with a partner, if she can help it. Or at least that's how she was once. She may have changed. The way she's glaring at me for having caught her tends to contradict that, though.

Well, if she thought I was going to leave her alone to fight off who knows how many bad guys on her own, while trying to save a girl, she has another thing coming. I didn't bring her back to New Orleans just to let her get killed by some two-bit drug-runner-turned-human-trafficker. I have important plans that require her being alive.

And I'd never forgive myself if she got hurt doing something she should have left to me. I spent years not forgiving myself for having let her go in the first place. I still remember the night she ran, and the hollow, stormy place she left inside me. I couldn't see or think straight, and I sure as hell couldn't come up with a plan. I knew she wouldn't have left unless she wanted to, which meant she'd chosen to do it the way she had.

Without me.

I hadn't been willing to face the humiliation of charging after her. I didn't chase women, and I sure as hell didn't go after girls who chose to leave me. So I never asked Camille where she'd gone. I didn't ask her father or Beau, and I cut off all forms of contact with her. Deleted her number. Erased her email addresses. Tried to erase her face from my mind.

And then I dove into New Orleans like a man possessed, trying to erase the memory of ever having loved her.

I couldn't do it. No matter how many glasses of gin I drank, no matter how much whiskey I burned through, I couldn't get her out of my head. And every other girl felt like lukewarm jello compared to Brooks, who was fire molded into a girl so beautiful it hurt your eyes to look at her.

I should have gone after her. And my subconscious never let me forget about it.

It was why I'd agreed to help her with her war in New York. That wasn't chivalry, because I was no fucking white night.

I'd wanted to assuage the guilt I'd carried since I let her go.

Though if I'm being honest with myself, I know I also wanted to be the man who finally saved her and made her stay.

Perhaps I'm more of a white knight than I realized.

All of which leads me back to the girl who is yet again getting herself into trouble without a plan for how to get back out again. Only this time, I'm not going to just stand by and watch it happen.

I glance up in time to see her eyes suddenly move from me to the parking lot behind me, and spin around to see two vans pulling in, their tires squealing and their drivers running over both curbs and small trees in their rush. They're spinning through the rain like the devil himself is after them, and I don't have to think twice to know they're doing something illegal.

Like kidnapping a girl.

Right. Time to play, then.

"What are you thinking?" I ask, dropping back into the

shadows next to her. They'll see my car if they're looking, but we're in a parking lot and I hope they won't think anything of it. We're sure to be outnumbered, and I don't want them discovering us any quicker than they have to.

She pulls her gun up and checks the magazine, the movements so smooth I wonder how many times she's practiced them, then turns to look at me, a knife between her teeth and a locked and loaded gun in her hand.

"You look like a fucking pirate," I breathe. More than that; she looks unbelievably sexy, her hair tousled and flying around her face and murder in her eyes. The knife is over the top, but the thought of her in some skimpy pirate wench outfit, the skirt too short and the top too tight, is making my cock twitch.

"You should talk," she snorts. "All you need is an eye patch and a parrot. You've already got the cane."

I move closer, feeling the heat of her against me, and let my lips travel to her ear. "And here I thought you didn't like my cane."

Goose bumps travel down her neck and across her jaw and I have to fight to keep from licking her. I want to taste the flesh right here, in this soft spot beneath her ear. One of the only soft spots she allows. I happen to know how ticklish she is right there, and how she gasps when you touch her right.

Devils, she must hate that I know that.

It brings a sly, curving grin to my face, and I lean a bit closer and let myself taste her. Just for a second.

She jerks away and stares at me like I'm insane. "Did you just *lick* me? We're about to start a gunfight and you thought you needed to remember what I taste like?"

"Oh love, I remember exactly how you taste. I'm just waiting for you to remember how much you liked it when I played that game."

Her face goes cold so suddenly that I miss the moment it changes.

"Are you going to help me or what? Because if you're not, then I suggest you get the hell out of my way."

She literally elbows me to the side, then pulls up her gun and runs forward, already shooting. I stare after her for a beat, trying to understand what she's doing, then take off after her, my cane tucked under my arm and two guns in my hands.

I guess we're not discussing a plan, then.

Typical Brooks.

***

The fight is quick and intense. Brooks kills the first two guys out of the first van, then spins and takes cover behind it, her eyes on the other van and the men getting out of it. They have guns in their hands and are already firing, and I slide to a stop next to my girl and try to fucking think. We don't know if anyone else is in the van we're hiding behind, or whether they even have the girl we evidently came for, and which van she might be in. If they have her, shooting in at either van could go all sorts of wrong. The last thing we want to do is kill her while we're trying to rescue her. We also don't want to kill all the men—not if we're going to try to kidnap one of them and force him to talk.

Though I don't know whether Brooks even remembers that she wanted to do that. She spins and takes two more shots, then comes back and reloads.

"Do you actually need me here at all?" I ask, half amused and half annoyed. I haven't gotten a shot off yet and she's already killed most of the guys.

She huffs. "Are you actually going to make yourself useful? Or just sit here and watch?"

This girl.

I hurl myself over her and roll when I hit the ground, coming up with my gun in front of me and taking out the first guy I see, then jump to my feet and run for the van, intent on finding the girl we're here for. When I slide the door open, though, the inside is empty, and I stare at it for a moment, confused and off balance.

Where's the girl we're rescuing?

Moments later I hear voices, and look up to see several girls stumbling out of the door that leads into the catacombs. They're dressed to the nines and wearing something sparkly over their faces, their hair long and curled, and I can tell from here that they've had far too much to drink.

I look from them to Brooks to find her eyes wide, and know she's coming to the same conclusion I am. They didn't have the girl, yet. They were coming to get her.

Seconds after that, another van comes screeching into the parking lot, and I don't have to look at it to know what's going on. The first two were either decoys or padding, and though we killed the guys driving them, we're not out of the woods, yet. Brooks and I both move at the same time, racing for the girls that just came through the door. She's shorter than I am, but she's sprinting like her life depends on it, her strides matching mine.

Almost like we were somehow born to run together.

I push that ridiculous thought out of my head and skid to a stop in front of the girls, who now look terrified.

"Sophia?" Brooks blurts out. "Sophia Wimbley?"

One of the girls looks at her, the terror on her face growing even deeper. "Yes. Why?" Her drawl is casual, her voice well-bred and highly educated.

Not from the mafia, then. This is one of the socialites. And I'm guessing that if Brooks knows her name, it means she was the mark tonight.

"Terrific," Brooks says, and suddenly she's a completely

different person. She's not the girl who was just shooting to kill, intent on protecting this girl with her life if she needed to. She's the girl's best friend. The one you see arm-in-arm with her friends at the mall, laughing and making eyes at the guys across the way. The transformation is so quick, so complete, that I do a double take, trying to figure out how she did it.

"Oh my God, thank God I found you," Brooks is babbling. "The thing is, we have a sort of situation here, and your dad doesn't want you to get involved. He says you've got something delicate coming up and need to maintain your reputation?"

"My wedding," the girl stammers. "I'm getting married to—"

Brooks grabs her and turns her the other way. "Exactly! He sent me to make sure nothing happened to destroy that, but we've run into some trouble. I'm thinking it's best if you get out of here. Can't have you getting shot right before your wedding."

"Oh, okay. What's your name again?"

"Sloane," Brooks says without skipping a beat. "Sloane Brennan. You can tell your dad I was here taking care of you. Go find a taxi and get home, hm? And take your friends with you."

The girl doesn't have a chance to answer before the other van skids to a halt. Brooks and I turn and start firing, and for all I know the girl and her friend disappear into thin air. I don't know and I don't care. I'm too busy trying to figure out how I'm going to get Brooks and myself out of this alive.

Five men jump out of the van, and now I think we're really in trouble. But then I see the glint of metal in the shadow of the wall on the other side of the parking lot, and remember the bike.

We have a motorcycle.

We can't get to my car—that van is between us and the black beast I brought here—but we have something better. And these guys don't know that we have it.

I grab Brooks' hand and sprint for the thing, counting on her to keep up, and she lays down cover as we run. She must hit at least one of the guys because I hear a body fall to the ground, but I'm too busy trying to plan our escape to pay too much attention. If we can get to the bike, I think we can make it out of here. Not through the parking lot, because those men will be able to follow us too quickly.

But through the catacombs.

We reach the bike without getting shot and I stick my hand out. "Keys!"

Brooks doesn't argue. She reaches into her jacket, yanks them out, and throws them at me, and within seconds I'm on the bike revving the engine. Brooks growls–probably because I'm not letting her drive–but then jumps onto the bike behind me and, after a moment of hesitation, wraps herself around me.

My cock immediately goes hard at the contact. She's hot, her breath on my neck and her hands low on my belly, and I have to fight the urge to push her against the wall and ravish her the way I want to. I want to tangle my hands in her hair and press my body against hers, tilt her head back and devour her mouth. Taste every fucking inch of her. I want her wrapped around me in a whole different way, and the lust of it is so strong it nearly knocks me flat. I haven't felt anything like this since...

Since...

Since the last time I had her in my bed at my father's mansion. I'd fucked her for hours, taking my time and making sure to touch every inch of her body. I'd wanted to brand her with my name, spread my scent across her like some sort of animal. I told her I loved her that night, and we went to sleep with her tangled up in my sheets and my body still half-covering her.

When I woke up, she was gone.

A gunshot brings me sharply out of the memory, and I realize Brooks is hissing in my ear.

"What are you doing, waiting for this to get *more* exciting? Get us the fuck out of here!"

I jerk back into reality. Shit, I'm about to get shot, and so is Brooks, and I'm sitting here daydreaming about her body.

I really need to start thinking about therapy.

I tuck my cane under my arm for safekeeping, pull her arms tighter around me, and take off through the parking lot toward the door into the catacombs.

This entrance has always been my favorite. Now I add another reason to the list.

***

We get back to my estate high on adrenaline and triumph, and that heady feeling of having survived something you know you shouldn't have survived. I let the bike drop to the ground in the driveway and pull Brooks into the house and up toward my bedroom.

I have things I need to discuss with her, and I don't want an audience.

For once, she doesn't argue, and follows me up the stairs and into the wing of the house that I call my own. We pass one door, then two, and I throw the third open when we get there. My suite spreads out in front of us, only sparely decorated, and I take only a moment to appreciate how quiet and clean it is in here.

When I turn to Brooks, she's leaning against the wall, her hair down and her eyes wide, the pupils blown out with the action of the night. And I can't help myself anymore. I dive into her, covering her mouth with mine and taking what I've wanted since I saw her in the catacombs a week ago. She's sweet and smoky and dark, the epitome of New Orleans, and just like the city, she opens up for me, tilting her head and welcoming me like she's been waiting for this. My tongue sweeps into her mouth and I feel her groan in my chest.

It rattles down my body directly to my dick, and I'm hard as a rock before she's finished.

I press against her, rocking my hips with driving, adrenaline-fueled need, the high of the night still humming in my veins, and Brooks gasps. She doesn't pull back, though. Instead, she spreads her legs further apart so my cock is nestled between them, two layers of fabric the only thing separating us. Our kiss becomes frantic, tongues and teeth clashing as we fight to get closer to each other, and I feel like I may have died and gone to heaven. Everything around me is singing with triumph at having her under my hands again, and the way she's reacting to me is stoking the fire in my veins.

I want to rip her clothes off, push her to the floor, and cover her with my body. I want to sink my cock into her and then lay there, savoring the feel of her around me before I fuck her. I'm going to claim her as my own and never let her go again, dammit.

This woman is mine, and it's time she fucking admits it.

In that moment, though, she pulls away from me and stares into my eyes. She's breathing hard, her chest moving up and down beneath mine, and her lips are already swollen with the passion of my kisses.

"You saved me," she breathes.

And it's so unexpected, so out of place, that it takes me out of the moment and back into the memory. Did I? I suppose I did, with the idea of taking the bike into the catacombs, but it's such a strange observation, and so un-Brooks-like, that it throws me off balance.

Still, I can't disappoint her by refusing to take credit.

"Of course I did. Did you expect anything less?"

A frown creases her brow and she stares into my eyes,

looking so hard I wonder what she's searching for. A different answer? What's going on here?

"You came after me. You didn't leave me alone," she whispers.

And now I'm positive I don't know what she's talking about, or what's going on here. I was ready to rip her clothes off and fuck her, and she's having some sort of existential crisis. She's also looking at me like I'm the most amazing thing she's ever seen, though, and I'm not going to stop her.

The truth is, I've had dreams about her looking at me like this.

I kind of like it.

The look disappears as quickly as it came, though, and her eyes blink and then turn serious.

"We have to figure out what we're going to do."

I almost fall down with the whiplash, but manage to keep myself on my feet, and agree with her quickly. We don't actually have time to fall to the floor and fuck all night, though it would be fun.

We're in the middle of destroying a human trafficking ring. And now multiple people have seen us and know we're involved.

Aislyn and the girls were already on a tight timeline, and now we probably are, too. Because it's only a matter of time before Dominick and whoever he's working for know that Brooks and I are trying to destroy their operation.

So I jump right in.

"Your father is the one running the ring, or at least coordinating it. He's running it out of Under the City. In the catacombs."

Her shock tells me that she didn't know at least some of that, but then she makes a face. "I already knew about my dad. I didn't know about the club, but that makes sense. But I now know the names of all those girls, and if I'm right, I also have locations for the kidnappings."

It's my turn now to make a face. "Okay, you win. That's better. But we need more. We need to know why. And who's ultimately calling the shots."

She nods, but doesn't look away from me. "And there's only one way to figure that out. Get inside."

Dammit.

"How did I know you were going to say that?" I ask softly.

"Because you know me better than almost anyone else in this world. Probably," she replies quietly.

The admission goes straight into my heart like an arrow, and I feel like I might die right then and there.

"And if you know that," I say firmly, "then you know I'm not risking you on some stupid plan." I push harder against her, pinning her to the wall and hoping she gets the message. I'm not letting her go. Not this time.

"I'm not yours to risk," she says simply. "Are you going to help me or what?"

I take a step back, my ardor turning to ice water in my veins. We were so close for a moment, there, and then she tore it away like a Band-Aid she never wanted to wear.

More fool I for thinking she'd changed.

"Maybe. How do you plan to get in?"

She gives me a Cheshire cat grin. "Easy. My dad's having a ball tomorrow night. And I'm invited."

13

BROOKS

The mansion I'm entering doesn't look like the mansion I know.

I mean, it's still gaudy and overblown. Gothic exterior with an interior that looks like it was designed by a French king. Or French prostitutes. But there are enough gas lamps in here to light up the entire block, and heating lamps placed in the corners as well. Those are unnecessary. The night is hot and humid, the air sticking to my skin as I walk through the front door and into the house itself.

I wonder, for a moment, who the hell talked my father into trying to heat the place in the middle of a New Orleans summer. But the thought is lost at the sight that greets me. Gone are the dark corners and spooky hallways of the house. Gone is the feeling that someone might be hiding behind the door, waiting to catch you doing something you're not supposed to. The place is done in elegant ribbons and garlands of magnolia blossoms. Bouquets cover every possible surface and the ceiling is drenched in silk stars on strings. Music is playing from somewhere—a real orchestra, if I'm guessing right—and everyone has a drink in their hand.

This is the mansion where I grew up, and yet it's wearing a mask, trying to be something it's not.

The air still tastes evil, though, and I shiver as it touches me. This place still holds bad things. It's just dressed up for the night.

I turn my attention to the people, now, and scan the crowd. Everyone is dressed to the nines and smells of money and power. I spot people I know from the underworld—the heads of families and their underlings, plus sons and daughters and wives. There are people I recognize from the society papers as well. Heads of industries—or what pass for industries in New Orleans—and those who have inherited wealth. Their faces are smooth and beautiful, their clothes expensive.

The people are also wearing masks.

I hiss at that. Of course my father didn't tell me this was a masquerade.

Why would he tell me the truth?

I slip to the side of the door, where I find a tray full of masks, and pick one up, holding it to my face. It's not fancy, but at least it allows me to fit in. I run my other hand down my dress, the deep green silk slippery against my palm, and feel the outline of the knife on my outer thigh. I wonder abruptly whether other people can see it—the material is clingier than I expected—and then realize that I don't care. Let them look. I *hope* they realize I'm armed.

I would have been stupid to walk in here without a weapon. I'm already regretting that I only have one, and that I'm here on my own. I thought it would be better to arrive alone, but now that I'm here and facing the crowd of people, where I'm sure traffickers are hiding in plain sight, I'm second-guessing myself. This whole thing smells suspicious. My father has never thrown balls, and I know from the research Camille gave me—and the questions I asked—that Dom Landry has more money than he's ever had. He's spending at an alarming rate and daring anyone to stop him, telling people that he has more protection than he did before.

Protection from who, though? And for what? Is he running the whole smuggling ring for someone, or is he just a stopping point on the journey?

Do they still use his basement to hold the girls they take?

I take one step forward, then another, finally moving into the crowd and looking to the left and right as I slide through them. The faces don't change. They're animated with laughter and drink, food and company. All of them speaking rapidly, and all of them masked. The masks don't hide their identities, however, and I have no trouble recognizing faces I've seen before.

I just don't know if I'll be able to identify any new faces again in the future. If the men my father works with are here and I see them, will I be able to name them if I see them again?

I'm not sure, and that makes me itch, like insects are crawling over my skin and I can't get to them. Lucien and I have nearly enough to start moving against my father out in the open, and potentially saving the girls he has, but we need to know what direction to take. I have to know who he's working with and where they're keeping the girls.

Of course, that's why I'm here tonight.

For the inside track.

Honestly, I'm surprised Lucien agreed to this plan in the first place. He's more cautious than I remember, more possessive. The swashbuckling pirate I knew when I was younger has given way to someone more charming and polished, but less reckless. Hell, he wouldn't have let me leave his house at all if I'd given him a choice.

Luckily, I didn't. Because he doesn't have the right to stop me. Not anymore.

I laugh to myself at the contradiction, well aware of how I'd sound to anyone else if I told them when I'm thinking. What I'm feeling. I'm furious at him for trying to keep me in his house and acting as if I belong to him, and angry at myself for the way my body reacts any time he's around. I hate that my feelings for him are still so sharp, and the way my eyes seek him out in any room, looking for him like he's some sort of security blanket.

I despise how relieved I was to see him last night in that parking lot. I don't want to think I need him. I don't even want to think I want him. Not after what he did.

But there's an idea running through my head that we fit together like two puzzle pieces, even after all this time, him moving to cover me when I turn and me filling in the blank space around his body when he pulls me to him. It feels like we should have been doing this our entire lives—like we *have* been —and like I wasted years of this potential by leaving.

I let myself catch on that thought momentarily, and then shake it off. None of that matters. I made the choice I made, and Lucien made his own choices, and there's nothing we can do about that now. We might be allies for the moment, but we live very different lives and once I save Aislyn, I'll head back to New York and my real friends.

I just have to take the next steps in my plan so I can do that.

Next steps that Lucien definitely won't like.

"Sister," a voice suddenly says in my ear.

I close my eyes, half in resignation and half in relief. I haven't seen Beau since the last time I left New Orleans, and although he could have tried to find me after I moved to New York, I'm equally to blame. Because I didn't try to find him.

For a long time, I also saw him as part of my father's plot to plant me in the Boudreaux operation and use me to undermine Gemini and Lucien, and after a lifetime of looking at him as a hero, that had been a big blow.

I still don't know for sure that he *wasn't* part of that plot, though, so when I turn to him, I'm hesitant.

He looks so much the same, though, that I have a moment of

utter whiplash. Same broad cheekbones and wide eyes, as dark as chocolate and twice as warm. Dark hair to match, and a mouth that wants to laugh more than it wants to frown. He's tall–as tall as Lucien, at least–and broader than he used to be. Five years older than me, Beau was the one I ran to when life got too scary, or when my father hurt me, and though I might have hated him for not protecting me from Dad, I never did. Beau had been a child as well, and incapable of doing anything to stop my father's temper.

Hell, I'd seen my dad go after Beau, too, and that had been worse than anything he ever did to me. I remembered the moment well. He had Beau tied up against the wall and was using a belt on him, leaving welts and cuts along my brother's back, and though Beau had been standing tight-lipped, not making a sound, my heart had shattered into a million pieces seeing it.

And then I put it back together, encased it with stone, and attacked my father, screaming at him to stop.

That had only gotten me in trouble, and I'd ended up forced to watch as my father punished my brother for me having said anything. A part of my soul had never recovered from that. But the armor around my heart only grew stronger. I learned to keep my feelings buried when they would be damaged, and to see things clearly when I needed to get shit done. And my relationship with Beau grew deeper than ever.

Then I ran for New York and left him behind.

So right now, seeing him for the first time in years, is like water to a woman dying of thirst.

I fly into his arms, screaming with laughter, and he catches me and holds me close, his heart hammering against my own and finding the same rhythm, the way it always has.

When he pushes me back to look at me, his grin is big enough to split his face. "You didn't even tell me you were in town."

"I haven't exactly had time," I said, laughing. "I just got here!"

He tips his head at that, though, and the smile melts away. "You haven't been here in years. I thought you were done with this place. What are you doing here? And why's your hair..."

He gestures vaguely to my hair, by which I guess he means to ask why it's red now instead of blond.

I answer the easiest question first.

"I decided I like it better red."

His eyes grow narrow. "And the rest?"

I pause for a moment, mind flying over the facts. How much can I tell him? Do I trust him? *Can* I trust him?

No, I realize. I want to, but I can't. Not until I know whose side he's on. Because if he's allied with my father, in the name of taking over the Landry family one day, it'll mean he knows about what Dad is doing.

"One of my friends in New York was kidnapped," I say, going for a partial truth, which will be easier to keep track of if he decides to question me. "And her trail led me here. I'm trying to find her, before..."

"Before....?" he asks.

God dammit, he's become better at hiding his feelings than he used to be. When we were kids, Beau couldn't keep a single secret from me. After so long, though, I don't know how to read him.

"Before anything happens to her," I say quietly, wondering. And then, on a gamble: "I'm afraid she might have been taken by human traffickers."

I watch him closely, intent on catching any change that might be due to guilt or knowledge. Anything that says he knows what I'm talking about. But his face remains neutral, with very slight shock.

"Trafficking? What makes you think so? Do you have any proof?"

I don't answer him. Because his response means he either doesn't know anything... or he's covering for my father. And if it's the latter, I can't afford to give him anything, on the off chance he passes it to Dad. I may have a plan, but I don't know where it's going to go yet, and I can't afford for my father to get wind of what I'm doing before I'm ready.

I already know how that would go, and it wouldn't be pretty. Daddy Dearest doesn't take well to what he considers betrayal, especially from family members who spent last night telling him they wanted to come back into the fold.

Beau stares at me for several intense moments before his face clears and he lets his mouth relax. He leans toward me, drops his voice, and says, "I love you, kid, and I don't want to see you get hurt. I'm not sure it's a good idea to keep looking for your friend. I'd rather see you get out while you still can."

He turns and leaves without saying anything else, and I watch him for a moment, left speechless at what he just said. Is he saying what I think he's saying?

Namely, that he knows exactly what I'm asking and is warning me to stop digging because it might not be good for my health.

Which would mean he knows what my father is doing.

And, if I'm not mistaken, thinks I might be a target.

I let that sink in for a moment, trying to wrap my head around it. I never would have imagined that Beau would be part of something like human trafficking, and I don't want to believe it. My brother is a good man and a hero, or at least he was when I knew him better. There's no way he'd stand by while something like this is happening.

Unless he's not supposed to know, and is working to undermine my father.

Like I am.

That thought brings a rush of excitement to my veins and I gasp, wondering if that's it. Beau's the heir to the organization, but that doesn't mean my father tells him everything. I wouldn't be surprised to learn that my father had certain rackets that he didn't tell Beau about, and sex trafficking is so illegal that I'm betting my father would hold it close to his chest. But what if Beau found out about it anyhow?

What if he saw or heard something like I did when I was young, and started doing research?

I haven't spoken to him since I left for New York, so he may have been working on this for years. And I like that version a whole lot better, because it matches with the man I want to think my brother is.

I let my eyes rove across the room, still thinking, but stop, surprised. I turn my eyes back to the girl I just passed over and stare at her, confused. I know that girl. I'm sure I do. But I can't think of where I know her *from*. Not school; I haven't attended school here since I was ten, and I doubt many of those girls are still in the area. Certainly not from any of my social circles; those consist of Camille, Camille, and Camille.

But she's familiar, and I feel like I just saw her yesterday.

Wait.

I did see her yesterday. Because she's one of the girls from the files Lucien gave me. She's one of the missing girls, and now that I've realized it, I see all the markers. She's young, probably only seventeen or so, blonde, and very pretty. Green eyes and a face full of freckles, though they come off as a charm rather than a flaw.

She's also the only person in the room not wearing a mask. And she looks miserable and very frightened.

I'm moving before I can think about it, my fancy dress swishing around my legs with my speed, and within moments I'm at her side. "Are you okay?" I ask, threading my arm through hers.

The girl looks up at me with a dazed, vacant look, and I add one more thing to the list of characteristics. She's been drugged. I don't know what they've given her but her pupils are blown and she looks like she doesn't know where she is. She does glance behind me, though, and I turn to see who she's looking at. An older gentleman—and I use the term loosely—who looks like Colonel Sanders. White suit, very southern, and a bushy mustache. Gray hair and glasses. He looks like he belongs in antebellum Georgia, and I immediately hate him. No one dresses like that anymore unless they believe in antiquated society and ideas.

Just looking at him makes me feel like a film of grease has been smeared over my skin.

I don't have to ask. I don't *want* to ask. The girl is shaking, now, and that can only mean one thing: That man hurt her in one way or another, and she's terrified of going back to him.

I know what I have to do.

I came here with a plan to get inside my father's operation and figure out what's going on, but I wasn't expecting to have a victim fall into my lap. Now that I have her, I'm not going to let her go again. I'll just have to find another way into the smuggling ring. I tighten my grip on the girl and turn toward the main doors of the house, praying we can get away before Colonel Sanders sees us. I tug gently on the girl—God, why can't I remember her name?—and start walking toward the exit. She resists at first, but once she sees where we're going she starts to walk faster, as if she just realized I might be taking her to freedom. The shaking stops and her breath becomes quicker, and I'm sure that if I looked at her, I'd see her eyes clearing.

She wants to get out of here, and that increases my need to do just that.

Before we've taken five steps, though, another man cuts right in front of us and stops, glaring down at us like he's just caught us trying to escape from jail.

Given what I suspect this girl is going through, he's not far off.

I look up at him, scowling and ready to tell him who I am and that he can fuck off, but stop when I see his eyes.

If the girl's eyes were hazy and unfocused, his are absolutely evil. Small and black, beady and glaring, they look like they belong on some sort of hateful animal rather than a human being. He looks at the girl like she's nothing more than a cockroach, and then turns his eyes to me. I narrow my own and shoot daggers at him with my eyeballs, but those daggers bounce right off what I'm sure must be lizard skin.

This man isn't human. He can't be.

When his eyes run up and down my body and his face turns thoughtful, I want to be sick.

"Where are you taking our girl, princess?" he asks.

His voice is gravelly and thick, and I want to smash his face in for the way he's looking at us. I fight to keep my voice level, though, and say, "She's not feeling well. I'm taking her out for some fresh air."

He chuckles, and it's the epitome of evil, and my fingers twitch for my knife.

"She doesn't get to go outside. Unless you want to take her place." His eyes rove up and down my body again, and I feel them like a physical touch.

When I don't answer, he just smirks and takes the girl from me. "I didn't think so."

He jerks her toward him and tucks her into his body, and when I glance at her face I can see a look of pure terror... and then the blank mask again. Her eyes stop glittering, her mouth goes slack.

Just like the girls in the hallway when I was a child.

I watch the man walk away with her, glaring at his back, and promising myself that at some point, I will save her. And then I'll slit his throat and watch him bleed out at my feet.

When I turn away, unable to watch the scene anymore, I find Lucien at the top of the stairs into the room, watching me. He catches my eye, takes in my face, and starts walking toward me.

14

LUCIEN

We stare at each other for a full five seconds, my foot poised above the first step to get to her, before she blinks and loses the horrified, scared look she was wearing. She puts her mask back up to her face, straightens her shoulders, and shakes her head at me.

It takes me several more seconds to understand what the fuck she's doing.

Then she turns from me and walks toward some guy holding drinks, acting like she didn't just have her arm around a trafficking victim who was then taken back to the man keeping her.

I watch her leave, letting my gaze move down her body and back up in appreciation. She's wearing deep green silk, in a design that walks a very fine line between elegant and showing too much skin. The dress clings to her in all the right places, accentuating her long legs and narrow hips. The sharp tuck of her waist. The bulge of her chest. The dress has no back, though, and I let my eyes slide up her bare skin, from the crack of her ass to the spot in the middle of her spine where a tattoo starts. It snakes its way up her back to twine around the base of her skull, and my fingers twitch with the need to trace it.

That's new, or at least didn't exist the last time I had my hands on her.

I want to lay her face-down on a bed and study it with my fingertips, and then my tongue. I want to know what it is and what it means and when she had it done. And then I want to spread her legs and take her while I stare at that fucking tattoo.

I snap my eyes back to her head, chastising myself for that thought, and continue my catalogue of her appearance. Her hair is up, but tendrils have fallen to curl along her neck and shoulders, and I saw enough of her face to know she did a smoky eye and bright red lipstick.

She's beautiful without a stitch of clothing on, and adding a fancy dress and well-done makeup makes her nearly irresistible. Which makes me incredibly uncomfortable in a room that almost definitely holds men who trade in girls that look just like Brooks.

I snatch a whiskey off a passing tray and bring it to my lips, finally taking the first step and starting to follow her. I don't know what she's playing at or why she motioned not to get near her, but I don't trust her. When I arrived, she had an arm around a girl and was talking to a man twice her size, and he was looking her up and down like she was nothing more than a chess piece he was considering buying.

And she was standing there letting him do it.

When he took the girl away from her, she didn't argue–or stab him, which was what I would have done. Instead, she watched them leave with a thoughtful expression. Like she was trying to figure out how to use the man and what he'd just done.

I growl to myself. She told me she was coming in here to get inside her father's organization, and then left without telling me what she meant by that, and now I'm going through the whole conversation again, looking for a clue. I'm worried she's come here to do something stupid without telling me, and before I have a plan or the men to execute it. I don't have to ask to know she's being reckless, just like she always is, and believing she can do more than she actually can.

I quicken my steps when she turns a corner and stride after her, unwilling to let her out of my sight for more than a few seconds for fear that when I get to where she should be, she'll be gone.

I do not look at my reasons for this, aside from the simple truth that she's playing with fire and is going to get burned, which will no doubt cost me time and money. Because I'll have to find her and save her instead of doing the research I want to be doing.

When I get to the corner, I find her just on the other side of it, leaning against a wall and gazing up at some man I've never seen before. She's looking up at him through her lashes and flirting like her life depends on it, and I very nearly pull my knife to murder the man before her eyes flash to mine and widen in warning.

Right.

No murdering.

Though I take in his face and memorize it for later, so I can find him when we're not in such a public place.

Brooks, meanwhile, is giggling–giggling!–like he's just said the funniest thing in the world, and I revise my plan. I'm not just going to murder him. I'm going to cut off his dick and shove it in his mouth, then skin him alive for daring to even look at her.

Not that I care who she talks to.

No, the problem is bigger than that. She's a beautiful girl at a party full of men who steal beautiful girls, and walking around like she owns the joint. This might be her father's mansion but she knows he's in on the smuggling ring, so that makes this place dangerous. And yet she's acting like nothing is going to touch her. I don't know what sort of life she's used to up in New

York, but down here there is no protection from the men we're chasing. People will shoot to kill. They won't care who she's related to or who's protecting her.

Hell, her father may have ordered her death if he think she's down here to make trouble for him.

I just need her to calm down for a moment. Five minutes. An hour. My men are out in the city finding Dom Landry's men and taking them into our dungeon for questioning. If she'll sit still for an hour, I'll be able to add to our bank of knowledge, and we can move through the party with better direction.

She might have a plan–hell, she's probably in the middle of it right now–but if it includes her going under cover with men who destroy girls for a living, I'm not going to allow it. Not until I have all the information and a way to get her back out again.

A voice in my head tells me firmly that it's not my call, because she's no longer my girl and hasn't shown any willingness to accept me as a protector. She's also never taken well to being ordered around, so I can't exactly pull her to the side and tell her to cool it until she gets my permission to carry on.

Though the thought of doing that brings a smile to my lips.

Brooks looks up, catches me smiling, and glares at me like she's just caught me having inappropriate thoughts about her.

In all fairness, she'd be right. Because half of me knows I don't have any right to her, but the other half is picturing grabbing her by the hair and dragging her away from that man. Finding a deserted closet and having my way with her.

I turn away from the scene, desperate to get my imagination under control, and catch sight of the man Brooks was talking to when I first arrived. The one who took the girl away from her and returned her to the man dressed like he's on his way to run a circus. He's staring at Brooks, his small, dark eyes intent and considering. He tilts his head with interest, and then nods. Seconds later he's gone, leaving nothing but the stink of a trafficker in his wake.

I don't like the way he was looking at Brooks.

I like even less that I suspect that to be part of the plan she hasn't told me about.

***

I shadow Brooks for another half hour, watching her flirt and drink with my fists clenched and my mouth sealed shut. I want to kill every fucking man in this room. Torture the men who've spent the night staring at her. I'm ready to outright slaughter the group that stands around Circus Man, watching her move around the room. It's clear that they've clocked her, and even more clear that they want her.

I want to tear their eyes from their heads and stomp them into oblivion. But I don't have any of my men here and though I'm reckless, I'm smart enough to know I'm only one man against ten. In a house that belongs to one of my many enemies.

So I keep my hands to myself and settle for glaring at Brooks, who is just as responsible for the situation as Captain Circus. Well. Maybe not *just* as responsible. The last time I checked, she wasn't subjecting innocent girls to smuggling and sex rings. But this is her game, now, and I'm not letting her get out of her share of the responsibility.

When she finally gets to the edge of the room, I take my chance and bulldoze through the crowd, grabbing her and pushing her out onto the patio.

"What are you doing?" she hisses, jerking her arm out of my grasp.

I don't let her put me off, though. I use my body to push her all the way to the railing and then keep going until she's bent backward over the stone balustrade.

"What are you complaining about? Given how you've been

acting all night, I figure you must like men who treat you rough."

The ice in her glare could freeze the blood in my veins, if I were fully human.

"I'm on a job and you know it. And you're blowing my cover right now."

I lean in and brush my lips over the column of her neck while my fingertips tickle along the top of her breasts. Her skin is silky and smooth. Hot, like she's got a furnace burning inside of her. And just like that, I remember what it's like to be inside her, her body squeezing me like she's trying to keep me there forever.

She is hot. And tight, and wet. And the memory drives me nearly out of my mind. Especially when she's putting herself in danger with men who will take advantage of that sort of thing.

"I suspect they just think I'm testing the merchandise," I breathe, letting my lips dance over her skin. "They probably see a potential buyer."

"I'm going to kill you," she says bluntly.

She doesn't reach for her knife, though, and that calls her bluff.

"Liar," I whisper. I drag my hand up the outside of her hip, find where she's stowed her knife, and chuckle. "Good girl."

I don't miss the gasp that bursts from her mouth at that, and I grin against her skin. So, Brooks has a good girl kink. I never would have guessed.

But it's good to know.

"Are you finished?" she finally asks, her voice breathy and weak.

My voice is husky when I answer, and I revel in the feel of my balls, tight and ready in my pants. My cock is hard as a rock, and I push it against her. This is a bad idea. A terrible idea. There are men in the room behind me that are on the verge of kidnapping her, and who are probably ready to kill me.

But I can't stop myself.

"This quickly? Not even remotely."

Her back arches, pushing her tits into my chest, and I nearly come undone right there. Every nerve in my body is screaming for her and I'm so hard I think I might die if I don't spread her legs and take her.

Then again, we're on full display on a balcony. In her father's house. And I'm a gentleman–or at least I play one for the city.

Sometimes.

I take a step back and breathe out, getting control of myself once again. Brooks straightens up and smooths her dress, and by the time she looks at me, she's got control of herself as well.

Pity. I'd like to turn her, bend her over the railing, and–

"I think my father and a partner are kidnapping girls and using them as escorts," she says bluntly. "Hiring them out to anyone who's willing to pay. Until the ship date."

Ice water hits me and I forget about my cock.

"And how long do they keep them here?"

"A week, max."

Shit.

"So that means..."

"We have three days to find Aislyn. And that's if she was the first one kidnapped for this load."

Three days. Worst case scenario. And that's generous, because Aislyn might have already shipped out.

"We've identified the ship that'll carry them out," I say quickly. "At least we think we have."

Her eyes flash. "Do you know who he's partnering with?"

"Not yet."

"Do you know for certain that the ship is the only way they're transporting them?"

Gods, she's too smart by half.

"No."

She closes her eyes like this is the worst news she's ever

heard, and my heart sinks. I'm working overtime and pulling information out of thin air, but it's still not enough. I don't know the things I need to know, and I didn't need her to tell me that.

But disappointing her feels like I've just failed at some very important part of life.

"Don't do it," I say quietly, knowing I sound more intense than I should.

When she opens her eyes, though, I see that she's already made up her mind. "I have to. We need to know exactly what's going on, and the only way we're going to find that out is if I'm on the inside."

I grasp her shoulders, trying and failing not to shake her. "No. We don't have a plan for that. I won't let you do it."

She reaches up and brushes a finger down my nose, but her eyes are cold and hard, and I know she's already made up her mind. She's going to do what she thinks she has to, to save those girls.

And it doesn't matter what I think of it.

"They're going to try to take me," she says quietly. "I made sure of it. They want fresh meat, and they think I'll bring a good price." She pauses, and for a moment her eyes grow gentle. "And you're going to let them."

I want to tell her I'll never let that happen, and that I'll kill any man who tries to lay hands on her. That I can't stand by while anyone else touches her or puts her in danger. I want to take her and force her into my car. Drive her home and keep her safe.

And I know I can't.

So instead, I think about the plan and what it'll bring us. She's right about getting on the inside. It's the only way to truly find out what's going on, and with luck, where it's happening. And she's the perfect target. Gorgeous. Young. Seemingly innocent.

Except she's not innocent at all.

And that might be the best part of the whole plan.

"We don't have a way to get you back out," I warn.

She shrugs. "I trust you to find me."

My heart expands so quickly I think I might have a heart attack. She trusts me.

She trusts me to find her.

I lean forward and wrap something around her wrist, then kiss her forehead. "They'll take your knife and any other weapon you have on you. They'll take your dress. But make sure you keep that."

I turn and leave before I can say anything else—like how fucking stupid this is—and trust her to do as I say. The hair tie has a tracking device embedded in it, and if she can keep it on her, I'll be able to see where she is at all times.

I'll be able to find her.

As I move back into the house, two of the men who've been following her all night brush past me, heading for Brooks. I hear a scuffle and a gasp, and then nothing, and I know they've got her. Probably a cloth soaked in ketamine to put her to sleep. Maybe chloroform. It doesn't matter, not really.

The only thing that matters is that they've got her, and I've got to let her go.

After all, this is the only way we'll get the information we need.

But I know I won't rest until I have her back in my arms.

I have three days.

I've been in worse situations, I remind myself. And this time, Brooks Landry is the prize for succeeding.

15

BROOKS

When I wake up, I'm still in the fancy dress I was wearing.

I am no longer in my father's mansion.

I sit up with a gasp, registering several things at once: I'm in some sort of room with a bunch of other girls, and it's far from the smoky, romantic gas lamps and gaudy decorations of my father's house. It's dank and dark down here, and though there's light coming from somewhere, it's not enough to see clearly. The air is close and humid, and I don't smell any hint of fresh breeze.

I run my hands quickly down my dress, making sure it's still intact, and realize it's damp. Not like I've been dunked in water, but like I've been through dark, musty air.

I reek of the catacombs.

The thought brings me to my feet and I look around the room, trying to collect as much information as I can. The walls are the dark, dripping stone of the underground tunnels and the air is close, just as I would expect.

I'm not only not in my father's mansion. I'm not even above ground. If I'm right, we're in some type of holding cell, and it's not on the surface. God, I don't even know if we're in the cata-combs proper. Moisture is running down the wall next to me and pooling on the floor, and though the tunnels are damp, I've never seen anything like this. I feel as though we're under a lake and the water is slowly winning the war against the ceiling above us.

That thought makes me want to throw up, though, and I put it away as quickly as I have it. Panicking isn't going to do me any good.

At that moment, I realize that my hand is on my hip, and there's nothing under my dress. My knife should be right there —the butterfly knife I always keep with me—but there's noth-ing. Just my skin.

I reach quickly for the other holster strapped to my knee and search for the gun I had, but that holster is also gone. My phone is gone, because whoever brought me here took my purse.

I have no weapons.

My hand goes quickly to the hair tie around my wrist, and that's intact, at least.

I'd feel a whole lot better if it was lethal. I never go anywhere without at least one weapon on me. Then again, I've never been kidnapped. I probably should have realized they weren't going to let me keep my things.

I turn my eyes to the girls around me, and start to take stock of the situation. They're all very young, and very scared. They're milling around the room, asking questions of each other like someone might have the answer to what's going on. Some of the girls are sobbing, some are handcuffed. Everyone is terrified, but some of them look more defiant than others.

Every one of them is too dressed up for a dripping room in the catacombs. Some have on fancy dresses, like me, and I wonder abruptly if we all came from the same party. I assumed my father had the ball to meet with his contacts, but what if it was more than that?

What if it was a way to gather high-society girls?

I start to push through the girls, looking at their faces and trying to figure out whether I recognize any of them. There were definitely other girls at that ball, but I wasn't looking at them. I was too busy watching the men watch me, and trying to determine where their alliances were. Who might be in charge of the ring we were trying to bust.

Aside from that first girl, any female in the room was just background noise, and now I'm kicking myself for not being more observant. I know better. I was there to do research and yet I only looked at half the people.

Stupid.

I do recognize some of these girls for different reasons, though. They weren't in the files Lucien gave me, but they've been in the newspapers since I got here. Society girls, out to party, who've had their pictures taken for the press. Daughters of politicians who were photographed doing appearances with their fathers. Daughters of lawyers and businessmen and even the mayor. These girls are the crème de la crème of New Orleans society. I start asking for names, and though most of the girls are too terrified to speak, some of them do. Laura Hannaby. Sasha Johns. Mika Collins.

Kate Fontenot.

I stop when I hear the name. I hadn't asked anyone, but someone had answered, and when I look up, I find the blazing black eyes of a girl I know. Her hair is as dark as her eyes, her face sharp and pointed like she's some sort of pixie, and I'd recognize that smirk in my sleep.

I fly to her—as well as I can, given the crowd—and take her in my arms, my mind rushing to catch up.

"Kate, what the actual fuck are you doing in here?"

She looks rough, and I look closer, wondering if she's okay. Her eyes are darkened by shadows and she's even paler than usual, which is saying something. I also see a bruise forming on her left cheekbone.

And she's the only girl in here wearing normal clothes. She looks like she was on a run to the market or something.

"Well I didn't come here on purpose, if that's what you're asking," she says wryly.

I have to smile at that, because Kate is one of the only people I know who could be in a situation like this and still crack jokes. She and Sloane would adore each other. Not that I've ever had them in the same space. Kate is one of my one and only adult friends in New Orleans, and used to be one of my first stops whenever I came back to town. Camille introduced me to her early on, and we've been fast friends ever since.

Honestly, I don't know how Camille even knows her. They certainly don't move in the same circles.

Kate is, to put it nicely, the daughter of one of my most infamous madames in New Orleans. If you want to be more blunt, you could say Kate's the daughter of the woman who runs the best meat markets in town. She's not the kind of person you want to make an enemy of, and she doesn't fit with the profile of the girls we've been looking at.

I grab her arm and pull her to the side of the room, intent on finding out what's going on. Is there more to this story than we realized?

Is her mother involved?

I don't want to think that. I've known Kitty Fontenot–yes, their names are almost the same–as long as I've known Kate, and I adore her. Big, boisterous, and not afraid of anyone, the woman lives her life the way she wants to, and has more respect for women than most people in the world. Despite the fact that she runs a business where they sell their own bodies. She takes care of her girls, makes sure they get the money and medical care they need, and I can't imagine her ever selling anyone into a smuggling ring.

Though lately I'm starting to think I don't read people as well as I once thought.

"What's going on?" I hiss, pulling Kate up against the wall. "What are you doing here? How long have you been in here? Do you know who runs this thing?"

She puts up a hand. "God, Brooks, one question at a time. I haven't slept in about three days and my brain's not moving as quickly as it used to. I don't know what's happening or who's running it but it's not hard to guess what 'it' is." She looks around the room and then back to me, her eyebrows lifted. "Do *you* know what's going on?"

"Probably more than you," I say, and give her the very short version of what we've discovered. "I went to a ball at my dad's house with Lucien and–"

She grabs my arm. "Lucien? Lucien Boudreaux?"

My heart sinks a little bit at the way she says his name, but I nod. "It's sort of a long story."

"I bet it is," she drawls, the corners of her mouth turning up. "You two never do anything the short or easy way."

"First of all, there's no 'us two' about it," I say firmly. "He just did me a favor, that's all. Loaned me a hundred men for a situation in New York, then decided to go up there to watch. When a friend was kidnapped he gave me some information about it, and when it looked like she was taken to New Orleans, I came down here to find her."

Kate's face is carefully blank. "With Lucien Boudreaux."

"Yes, that's what I just said."

"Lucien Boudreaux loaned you one hundred men and went to fight a war with you, then happened to have the information you needed, and then flew you down to New Orleans at the drop of a hat. Just being Johnny on the Spot."

I stare at her for a beat, confused. "Evidently."

Then I see her mouth twitch. "And he's still sticking to the story that you two are just friends?"

"I wouldn't even call it friends, honestly," I snap, annoyed at this game. "He tried to lock me up in his house so he could do all the groundwork."

Kate tries not to grin at this. She fails. "Lock you up in his house? You're... staying at his house?"

At that point, I've finally had enough. "Kate, I don't have time for you to play around. Lucien and I aren't whatever you're thinking. We're barely anything. I haven't even fucking talked to him in years. The only reason I'm at his house is that we're working on this case together. Now how the fuck did you get here?"

She finally stops smirking and grows serious. "Made a mistake. Saw a girl getting roughed up outside a club and went to help her. Three guys were trying to grab her and her friends, and I wasn't having it. But they had guns and knives and I was unarmed, so..."

"So they just took you too?" I gasp, surprised. This doesn't sound like anything we have in our files, and it goes against the idea that they're only taking girls from rich families. Kate's mother is influential, sure, but she doesn't exactly travel in high New Orleans society.

"Yep. Been here three days."

Three days. If that's true, she was here almost from the start of this group.

Which means we only have four days until this group is shipped out.

"Were there many other girls here when you arrived?" I ask quickly.

She looks at me like I've lost my mind. "Sure, they were down here having a big party."

"Kate, I'm serious. This is important."

She tips her head, but then sees that I'm serious. "Right. No, when I got here there were only a couple other girls. But it's been filling up since then." She pauses and watches my reaction, then bites her lip. "That's not good news, is it? That means something bad."

God, I don't know how to tell her this without sounding dramatic. Then again, this is a dramatic situation. Maybe I shouldn't sugarcoat it. "It just matches what we thought. We're guessing this group brings girls in waves. Collects them for about a week, one or two at a time, and not only from New Orleans. They're getting them in New York, Boston, Atlanta..."

"Why?" she breathes. "For what?"

I meet her eyes and grit my teeth. "They pass them out as escorts while they have them, then ship them somewhere. We don't know where, yet."

Kate closes her eyes and then nods. "Right. Of course they do. And there's a timeline."

"Exactly."

When she opens her eyes again, they're full of knowledge. And determination. "How much time do we have?"

Right. Moment of truth. "If you've been here three days? We have three days until the ship date. Four at the most."

Her face goes even paler, but I don't see any fear in her eyes. Instead, she gives me a sharp, brittle grin. "Then I guess we better find a way to bust the hell out of here and save these girls. That why you're here?"

God, I want to hug her. "That's exactly why we're here."

What I don't tell her is that I'm here without a fucking plan, and without a team behind me. Sure, Lucien is above ground and will give me anything I need, but he might not know where the fuck I currently am—I don't know if this tracking device even works—and I'm guessing he can't get to me. And because I left without drawing up a plan with him, I'm essentially flying solo.

And for the first time in my life, I don't have a backup plan. I'm trapped in an underground room with a bunch of very scared girls, and I don't know if Lucien can track me.

I don't know if he's coming to save me. Or not.

I've had a lot of bad ideas in my time, and I've even acted on some of them. Hell, sending Dante into Dax Romano's world to spy for us was one of the dimmest things I've ever done, though it seemed like a good idea at the time.

But I'm starting to think that this right here–coming down here without a plan or way to communicate with Lucien about what's going on–might be the stupidest thing I've ever done.

Even worse, I don't see Aislyn in this room.

I got myself kidnapped and thrown into a holding cell with a bunch of helpless girls, and the girl I'm looking for isn't even here.

16

LUCIEN

I shove the doors of the warehouse open and storm through them, my men following me with our prisoner.

"Put him on the wall," I snarl.

I'm beyond angry. Brooks has been missing for twenty-four hours and I haven't been able to find anything about where she might be. I gave the kidnappers ten minutes, just so they wouldn't realize I'd known what they were going to do, and then I tore through the ball, looking for any sign of Brooks or the men who'd taken her.

But everyone had disappeared. The captain of the circus. The man who'd been following Brooks. I didn't see the girl Brooks had been talking to or the men who'd shoved past me to get to her, either.

I couldn't even find Dom Landry, which was strange, considering it was his party. I'd seen Beau Landry momentarily, but he'd looked harried and upset, and had been on his way out the door.

And since then... Nothing. No one was talking. My contacts didn't know anything, and if they did, they weren't sharing.

Brooks was caught in a smuggling ring, being held captive in some dank, dark cell somewhere, and I was up here fighting to get someone to tell me something I could use.

Enter Simon leBanc.

I turn and glare at him now, so angry I can hardly see straight.

"You're sure this guy knows where she is?"

Simon turns large, frightened eyes from me to the man now handcuffed to the wall of the warehouse, and nods once. "He sure does. He's one of their main guys."

"And how the hell were you able to get to him?"

Some of Simon's fear melts at that and he gives me a cocky grin. "I've been working for them for a while. Turns out they trusted me more than they should have."

I almost laugh at that, because it's a level of self-awareness that I never would have expected from a freelancer like Simon. Though he's right. Whoever hired him was fucking stupid to think he'd have any loyalty to the organization. He's an outlaw. Doesn't belong to any one family and goes wherever the wind takes him.

Or where the money's better.

I cleaned out an entire set of stock holdings to make sure I was paying him more than Landry's organization. And in return, he gave me the name and location of the highest-placed man he knew. Simon himself doesn't know anything, of course. He's just a set of eyes, in charge of figuring out a girl's schedule for easier kidnapping. But he reported to some of the snatchers, and those men reported to the guy in charge of organizing it all.

That guy is now chained with his hands above his head in my warehouse.

And I'm going to do whatever it takes to find out what he knows, and where Brooks is.

"James Saldana," I say, strolling slowly toward the man. "You work for Dominick Landry?"

He narrows his eyes and glares at me. "I don't know who the fuck you're talking about."

"Right." I brace a hand on the wall near his head and lean toward him. "Then who *do* you work for? Let's start there."

Instead of answering, the man spits in my face.

He actually spits. In. My. Face.

I jerk back, disgusted, and then, before I can stop myself, I hit him right in the mouth. His head jerks back and hits the wall, and I feel a disturbing sense of vindication at the sound of it.

"That was rude, James," I say quietly. "Let's try this again. And I'll warn you right now: I'm going to start nicely. But if you don't tell me what you know, this is going to get ugly."

The man just grins. "Bring it on, Boudreaux. You don't have the balls to do anything I haven't experienced before. This isn't one of your little gambling dens."

This guy.

"So skipping right over the nice part, then?" I ask, forcing myself to be polite and polished. I can't say I'm surprised at his statement. People around here tend to think I'm more of a gentleman than I am. Someone who doesn't like to get his hands dirty. Maybe it's the way I dress, or the fact that I make my money at card games and roulette tables. Could be the fact that I don't run in any of the street gangs, like so many of the mafia kids do these days.

Or maybe it's the cane.

Without another thought, I toss my cane up in the air, catch it, pull the blade out of it, and swipe it through the air, the metal whistling as it flies. My aim is perfect, and by the time I stop the swing, James' left hand is laying on the floor.

He doesn't even realize what's happened until he looks down and sees it there.

Then he starts screaming.

"I think you'll find, James," I say, pushing my rapier back

into the cane, "that I'm capable of a lot more than people realize. And I'm willing to use every single skill in my repertoire to
get the answers I want. Now tell me what kind of ring this is
and how many girls are involved."

It's not the question I want to ask. I want to ask where the
fuck Brooks is and how I can get her out. But if I jump right into
that, he'll know how valuable she is, and at this point I'm
praying they don't realize she's related to Dom Landry. The
moment they do, she becomes worth more, and that means
she'll be in even bigger danger.

I have to play it cool, no matter how much it kills me.

"Fuck you," James hisses. "I'm not telling you anything."

Well, this is interesting. I thought this guy was a manager,
not a soldier. Not someone who'd keep his mouth shut in the
face of torture. How much was Dom paying him to inspire such
loyalty?

"Is that so?" I ask, letting my surprise show on my face. "In
that case, I guess we need to keep going."

I pull a butterfly knife from my pocket and whip it open,
then press it to his cheek. "What do you think, Daniel, the mark
of the devil, or the mark of Boudreaux?"

"Boudreaux," Daniel growls. "This family will last a whole
lot longer than the devil."

"Good call," I say thoughtfully. "And I wouldn't want to acci-
dentally summon Satan himself by drawing his mark in blood." I
place the tip of my knife into Daniel's cheek, press it in deep
enough to draw blood, and start carving our family crest into his
flesh as he screams.

And I think of Brooks as I do it with her favorite type of
knife. And I wonder where the fuck the girl is and how I'm
going to get her. Because every minute in that ring is a minute
too long. I don't even have time to stand around torturing
James.

But I don't know how else to get the information I need.

***

An hour later, James is dead, having given us very little to work on. When I mentioned Brooks, too jittery to keep her a secret any longer, he'd laughed at me.

"Brooks Landry? That red-haired bitch? Oh, we know her. We took her on purpose. With that last name, she'll bring even more than the rest."

"And you don't care that she's your boss' daughter?" I asked, shocked at his sudden candor.

"Care? Why would I care?" he sneered. "Dominick *told* us to take her."

I'd stabbed him then. Again and again. And then I slit his throat and let him fall gurgling to the floor as his life drained out of him. I was furious. So angry I could hardly see straight. My girl was in there fighting for her life–or at least risking it–and the man not only wouldn't tell me where she was, but laughed when I demanded to know.

And then he said her own fucking father had recommended her as a mark.

I couldn't believe what I was hearing. What father wanted that for his own daughter? What father knew what he was sending her into, and then did it anyhow?

True, Dom and Brooks have never had a good relationship. I don't know all the facts, but I know he hit her more than once–tried to kill her when she found out too much about him, if the rumors are true–and that she started carrying her first knife just to protect herself from him. I know Beau tried to protect her for a long time, until he realized he was too small to take on his dad.

And if Camille told me the truth when I asked, Dominick was the reason Brooks left New Orleans entirely.

From the sounds of it, Dominick is still abusing Brooks. He's just found a new way to do it.

I growl and punch the wall, frustrated at the fact that I still don't have anything to go on. Brooks is in danger, we're only two to three days from the ship date, and I don't have any way to reach her. I don't even know where to start looking.

Then I realize that I might have a way of finding out.

"Do we have his phone?" I ask, spinning to look at Daniel.

He cocks his head, but then pulls the phone out of his pocket. "I doubt he has numbers for anyone saved in here, boss," he says, handing it to me. "No one in their right mind would save something like that."

"I don't need numbers," I say holding the phone up to James' face to unlock it. "Take a picture of his face. Close as you can get." I turn away from the dead man, my fingers busy on the phone as I open up the settings and go to his GPS history. If this guy is in the ring and is as important as Simon claims, he'll have been to some important locations. Including, I hope, the distribution centers where they're holding the girls.

I might be able to find Brooks without having to kill anyone else.

Though I'll kill an entire army if I have to.

I'll kill anyone who gets in between me and my girl, and I'll do it so fast they don't even see it coming.

"What do you have, boss?" Daniel asks.

"His GPS history. We're about to do a tour of the city and figure out where their distribution centers are."

True, the GPS locations might not be as specific as I'd like, but they'll give me a place to start searching. And I've known this town a long time. If I can get into the right neighborhoods, I'll find people there to help me.

By hook or by crook. By threats or by money.

I don't care.

"Gear up," I say. "We've got a couple days. And I want her out."

17

BROOKS

The room is everything you'd expect from a smuggling ring, and yet the opposite of what I've experienced up to this point. For the last twenty-four hours—from what I can tell—we've been held in dark, dank cells that I believe must be underground. Under a lake or river, potentially, given how much moisture there is down there. My skin is sticky and saturated, my lungs heavy, and I feel like I've been underwater for the last day. Without adequate oxygen.

A couple hours ago, half the girls in that underground dungeon were gathered up and moved, though, including both Kate and me, and now we find ourselves in what looks like a 70s-style whore house. Not that I know what that looked like. But if I had to guess, this is what I'd think. Velvet-lined walls, chaise lounges, lots of beading and tassels. The place even has shag carpeting. At least I think that's what this is. It's not brighter, per se, because the colors and fabric are all so heavy.

But it's easier to breathe.

Or it would be if I didn't feel like this was some sort of escalation. I just didn't know what we were staging for. Yet.

"What do you think this place is?" Kate asks from her place next to me against the wall.

"I have absolutely no idea," I answer. "But I don't like it."

"Right," Kate murmurs.

She eyes the crowd of girls in front of us, all of them milling around with hopeless, vacant looks on their faces, and shakes her head. "They look like zombies."

"Hard to blame them," I reply. "They've been through hell and back already, and don't have any way out. And these aren't exactly girls who've been taught to fend for themselves."

It's one of the things I noticed right away, and something that makes me think the organizers of this ring are even smarter than we realized. These aren't just rich, entitled girls, being sold to the highest bidder and then dangled out in public so their family has to see them being used as toys. These are girls who've never had to do anything for themselves. They don't know how to shop or clean the house on their own, and they sure as hell don't know how to defend themselves.

In short, when kidnapped and put into a stressful situation, they don't know how to react because they don't have the right tools. Instead, they shut down and become pliant. And that plays right into their kidnappers' hands.

A man walks by and shoves two paper cups at Kate and me, barking that it's time to take our medicine, and this has become nearly as routine as the rest of the girls wandering aimlessly through whatever room we're in.

Kate and I don't fit the mold. We're not walking around like we've already died, nor are we following orders as seamlessly as the girls. We're talking back. Telling them no.

Actively planning a rebellion.

And as such, they've started trying to drug us.

It's not working, of course.

Kate and I both tip the cups to look like we're taking the meds, and I quickly hide the pills under my tongue. You know, that trick you learned in school when you didn't want the teacher to know you were chewing gum. It's harder with pills because they taste terrible and are solid, and therefore harder to hide, but these guards don't seem to have much interest in actually checking to make sure we've swallowed.

Given their industry, you'd think they would be more concerned with swallowing, but what do I know.

The problem with this process is that we have to get the pills back out of our mouths before they start to dissolve. We watch the man intently as he walks along the wall, checking the other girls to make sure they're adequately docile. As soon as he turns the corner, we both spit the pills back into our hands and put them in the pockets of the trousers we've been given. As soon as we have a moment alone, we'll use the brick we found to crush the pills into dust.

Right now, though, I'm intent on watching the changing of the guards and trying to figure out what we're going to do.

"So let me get this straight," Kate suddenly says, like her mind is moving along the same path as mine. "Your friend went missing and Lucien happened to be in New York, and happened to have information on said friend."

"Not her specifically," I correct, my eyes on the guard that just came into the room. He's heading for the office that's attached to this space, and I want to see how he gets in there.

"Right," Kate says wryly. "But still, Lucien has information. He says he thinks it's all going down in New Orleans and that you need to come home with him."

"Not with him. I mean, not specifically."

"Of course, not specifically."

She's grinning, but I ignore it. The guard is close to the office, now.

"And then he tries to lock you in his house to protect you. Instead, you break out, do a bunch of research, and then head to your dad's house to try to corner him into telling you something. You end up at this ball, where you meet Colonel Sanders, and you decide it's a good idea to get caught yourself so you can figure out..."

"Where this all leads," I say, finally turning my eyes to her. "We can't find an exact ship date or where they're sending girls or who's running it. And we need to know that if we're going to stop it."

She bites her lip. "And yet you came in here without a fucking plan to get back out again. Even if you get that information. And Lucien has no idea where you are or how to save you."

My blood freezes at hearing it laid out so plainly, but she's not saying anything I don't already know. I made a mistake coming in here without a plan, and an even bigger mistake not discussing it with Lucien first. I thought I could handle it, but now that I'm here, without my weapons or any way to communicate with anyone, I'm thinking I was beyond stupid.

I didn't even realize I expected Lucien to be my safety net until I cut him out of the picture. And now that he's absent, I feel like the ground has disappeared from under my feet. Like the world has turned sideways on me and I don't know how to fix it.

And I'm sure there's some deeper meaning there, if I want to look for it. Something that says 'Brooks, you've always been able to do whatever you wanted because you knew that at the end of the day, you could run home to Lucien and he'd help you out of the jam.' The problem is, I'm starting to think that's the truth. Just look at how he reacted when I asked him for men to take to New York with me. He barely even blinked an eye. Simply made the deal for how we were going to get his guys up north.

To fight my battles.

Just like I knew he would.

It brings a surge of emotion crawling up the back of my throat, and I swallow hard. I haven't thought deeply about my feelings for Lucien in a very long time. Honestly, I'm not sure

I've ever thought deeply about them. He's just the guy who's had his hand on my lower back, supporting me, since I was twelve.

Now that hand is gone and I'm not even sure it's still available. What if he hasn't come because something has happened to him? What if he came after me but my father's men caught him and he's now dead?

What if the last thing I said to him was that he needed to stay out of my way while I conducted a plan I hadn't bothered to tell him about?

I gulp... and push the thought aside. I don't know how I feel about Lucien, and this is not the time to sort that out. I'm sure he's fine. I'm just stressed and overreacting.

I've never experienced that before, but I've heard it happens.

And in the meantime...

I come back into reality just in time to see the guard I've been watching get to the office. He puts his palm on the pad to the side of the door—this ring is evidently a big fan of tech—and the door unlocks. Shit. That's going to be hard to replicate without a guard's hand, and I don't have time to replicate that sort of thing. I also don't want to kill someone and chop their hand off.

Pretty sure that would draw the attention of the other guards.

But I've been watching these guys long enough to know they're sloppy, and the guy who just went into the office is one of the worst offenders.

I watch, my breath catching in my lungs, and wait a few seconds, and for possibly the first time in my life I send a prayer out to universe. Please let something go right for me, please let something go right for me.

It does. When he leaves the office a few seconds later, he doesn't close the door all the way. It's still on the latch, and that means it didn't lock.

Go time.

"All that aside," I mutter to Kate, who's watching me, waiting for a response. "How do you feel about a little recon?"

Her face goes from judgmental to impressed to suspicious in half a second. "What do you mean?"

I nod toward the office. "Any room that has a hand scanner is bound to have interesting things in it, don't you think?"

She turns and looks, and a grin spreads over her face. "You mean like computers with things like ship dates and possible destinations?"

"And buyers and investors and even high-level owners of the ring," I confirm. "You interested?"

She huffs out a low, sinister laugh. "Brooks, you've known me a long time. Have I ever said no to a little bit of good trouble?"

"A girl after my own heart," I murmur. "Let's go."

We move toward the office, keeping our motions slow and as subtle as possible, and when we get there, I motion for Kate to wait outside while I go in and see what I can find. She nods once and then turns her back, moving in front of me to give me some cover while I slip through the door. It's so easy I wonder for a moment if we've been set up, and glance up into the corners of the room to see whether there are cameras in here.

There aren't. Of course there aren't. They would never expect those poor, defeated girls out there to do something like break into an office.

Of course, they also aren't expecting people like Kate and me.

I glance around the room, wondering where to start, and see that it's very plain. One desk. One computer. One chair.

"They must have saved all the gaudy decorations for the girls," I say, already moving for the computer. This group seems to have pretty good tech, from what I've seen, but they're also from New Orleans, and I've spent the last eighteen years living in either New York or LA.

I'm betting I know more about breaking into computers than they do about protecting them.

In the end, it's ludicrously easy. They don't even have the thing password-protected. I boot it up and stare at the desktop, shocked at how easy it was to get in. Then I start researching. The files are clearly labeled: a list of girls, a list of buyers, a list of possible destinations. And, importantly, a list of the ships that take the girls out of here. Dates, ship names, shipping manifests.

I open up the list of girls first and scan it for Aislyn. I've been looking for her since I arrived, and still haven't found her, and that bothers me. Has she already shipped out? Am I too late?

But her name is on the list, and the column marked for 'exported' isn't checked yet. She's here somewhere. I just have to find her.

I scan the list of buyers and destinations, but without my phone or even a pen or pencil, I have no way of recording anything. I do a quick search in the drawers but don't find a thumb drive anywhere, and even if I did, I don't know how I'd hide it. I'll just have to hope my memory is up to the challenge of holding onto the information I'm looking at.

Finally I go to the list with the ship names and manifests. I need to know how much longer I have before I'm in real trouble.

The news there isn't good. It looks like they do ship out once a week, on a fairly regular schedule. One hundred girls per ship, which explains why they've expanded to other cities. They must be going through the girls in New Orleans pretty quickly. The list of buyers gave me more information, though. They're not just selling the girls internationally. They're selling them in this city, too, as high-end escorts and pets.

They're making sure their families see them acting the slave to other men.

I don't puzzle over that one for too long, because a short knock on the door tells me I'm nearly out of time.

I go back to the shipping list and look for the next ship date, then count backward on my fingers to figure out what it means. I think I've been underground for twenty-four hours, which means it's been three days since I got to New Orleans. Six days since Aislyn was kidnapped. And she hasn't been shipped yet, which means she was definitely one of the first girls for the current group.

I glance at the date in that next row, and my blood turns to ice in my veins.

If my calendar is right, and this manifest is correct, then I'm already in more trouble than I realized. I've done my math wrong somewhere. Or maybe they're changing the schedule.

Because according to this, we ship out tomorrow night.

***

When I slide back out into the main room, I find that things out here have escalated. There are several guards in the room, and they're conducting what I can only describe as assessments on the girls. Each girl is led in front of two guards and told to strip down in front of them. Once they're naked, they're checked for any scars or imperfections. They're pinched and poked at like cows at a market.

And then they're told to spread their legs.

The guards are sliding their fingers against their pussies, and then inside them, to see how they'll react. They're taking their time on this part, too. Saying they're doing their research and making sure the girls will sell. Their laughs are ugly and wicked, and I'm already curling my hands into fists, ready to kill each of them.

The girls have woken up enough to know what's going on. And they're sobbing.

I watch, not sure what to even do about this. I have no weapons. I have no allies other than Kate. I'm entirely at their mercy, and this is a position I've never been in before. I hate it. I want to scream and kick and fight, and though I'm not sure how much good it will even do, I realize that I have to follow my instincts.

"Are you ready for this?" I mutter to Kate.

"Being felt up by the guards? No. I hope you're talking about something a little more brilliant than that."

I am.

"Follow my lead."

I make for the guard feeling up the girl before anyone realizes I'm moving, and tackle him from behind. He was enjoying his work and not expecting an attack, so he's entirely relaxed, and that makes it easy to crawl his back and get into position. I grab his chin in one hand and the back of his head in the other, and jerk with all my might.

His neck snaps like I hoped it would, and he falls to the ground, dead.

I'm already moving for another guard, intent on taking him out too, and out of the corner of my eye I can see that Kate's already dispatched one on her own. Before I can get to the next guard, though, someone grabs me from behind, yanks my hands behind my back, and jerks me backward.

"Looks like we've got a live one here," my captor mutters. "What's the move, boss?"

A voice I haven't heard before chuckles, and it drives chills down my spine. "Send her and the other bitch to Canal Street. No need to inspect them. I know who they are, and they'll bring top dollar no matter how soiled they are."

I'm shoved forward and have time to meet Kate's eyes, registering her sudden flash of fear, before we're pushed out the door and into the hallway, on our way to Canal Street. Whatever that means.

It's big trouble, I know that much.

Because I have no idea what to expect there.

And I now know that I only have a day to get the fuck out of this noose before I'm sold and shipped to who knows where.

God, I hope Lucien's doing something brilliant and sneaky that will get me out of here. I hope he realizes how quickly he has to move to save me—and Aislyn, wherever she is. And Kate, and all the girls I now feel responsible for.

I hope to fuck he's not dead.

18

LUCIEN

"Canal Street," Daniel mutters, the disgust clear in his voice.

I don't have time to ask him why he's sneering, but I do anyhow. "You don't like Canal Street?"

The sneer on his face becomes more pronounced. "It's not real New Orleans," he says quietly. "Might as well be Las Vegas."

I wonder now if Daniel has ever actually been to Las Vegas, because Canal Street is nothing like that monstrosity. On the dividing line between the Vieux Carre, where the Spanish and French lived, and the area where Americans decided to set up shop, Canal Street was, at one point, supposed to be an actual canal. I wonder if the city planners thought that would keep the Cajun section of society from attacking the American side.

I doubt it. The planners of this city never had much forethought.

More likely they thought it would be good to contain all the evils New Orleans has ever held–whore houses, dance halls, gambling dens, and opium joints–and would give all people an equal shot at wasting their money.

Maybe Daniel's right. That does sound like Vegas.

It also makes this area the perfect place to house a sex trafficking ring, though I can't for the life of me understand how anyone would keep it in the dark if they were doing it here, where all eyes are wide and staring. Canal Street isn't the seedy neighborhood it once was. These days, it houses a lot of retail and some newly renovated movie theaters. Trolleys line the streets and there's a parade every other day. Tourists crowd the sidewalks, eating as many beignets as they can hold.

Boudreaux has several casinos on this strip, but they don't open until midnight, because that's the only way to make sure no one sees what you're doing.

Who the fuck would try to smuggle girls through a building here?

Still, this was one of the most popular places on James' GPS, and I don't think he was coming here for fun. No one visits the same dance hall that many times each day. So there must be something. I just have to figure out what it is.

I stare up at the old-fashioned building in front of me, its wooden plans painted a garish color of bubblegum pink, with sea green trim along the corners and the roof. The place looks like a candy store just threw up on it, and I feel myself sneering. A dance hall, and an old-fashioned one at that. The place looks like it was renovated recently, but kept its original job. Instead of turning it into a club or bar, whoever owns it maintained it, according to the sign, as a dance hall. One large room where everyone can go dance, drink, flirt, and generally have a good time.

Back in the day, dance halls doubled as lounges where you could find prostitutes, and I've heard rumors that these days, they cater to a much more permanent version of sex slavery.

Like selling girls?

Maybe.

I walk to the front door of the place, my eyes on the guard standing there.

"Hall's not open yet, mister," he says gruffly.

I wouldn't expect it to be, and this strengthens my suspicions. After all, places that are doing illegal business won't want to be open during the day.

"What time does it open?" I ask.

"Nine, and not a second before. But it's not open tonight," he grunts.

This sets my teeth on edge, and I tap my cane once. "Doesn't make much sense to have a dance hall that's not open," I observe, trying to stay calm. What the fuck is this place, and what does it have to do with Landry's operation?

And why is it closed the moment I appear on the scene?

The man doesn't respond to my observation but lifts one shoulder in a shrug, and no matter how many additional questions I ask, he's evidently finished communicating with me.

Frustrated, I turn from him, trying to figure out who else I can ask. I spot Mrs. Fontenot, the biggest madame in town, strolling down the street, and approach her, but she takes one look at me and shakes her head, then actually tells me to get lost.

"Kitty—" I start, shocked.

She throws up a hand to warn me away. "Leave me alone, Lucien. I've got more important things to worry about than some Boudreaux looking for a place to get his dick wet."

I'm offended at the insinuation, but the woman is obviously out of her mind over something, so I let her go and turn around, looking for someone else. If I know anything about New Orleans, it's that the locals always know the business of everyone around them. They're either involved or have been told to stay the fuck away, and that has guaranteed that they do their research and figure out what's going on. If that dance hall is doing anything illegal, the street walkers will know about it.

And they're always desperate for money.

I see a girl within moments, and though she looks like she's doing okay–no broken teeth, and fairly clean–I'm also banking on her being open to bribery.

I mean, who isn't?

It only takes $20 to get her talking.

"That dance hall doesn't have any dances," she says quickly. "And we're never invited in. They sell other girls there."

"Other girls?" I ask sharply. "What does that mean?"

She looks at me like she's never met anyone so naive, which is a real laugh, considering she looks about ten years younger than me.

"The girls they have in there don't want to be there, mister. They've not agreed to live the life."

"English, girl," I growl. "I don't speak street walker."

This earns me a dirty look, but I sweeten her up with another $20 and she keeps talking.

"Once a week they hold auctions in there," she says, her voice lower and her eyes darting around the street like someone might be listening to our conversation. "High-end girls. Girls from good families. They ain't agreed to it, sir. They're sobbing and fighting. But they're bought by men who can afford that sort of thing."

Now my voice is just as quiet as hers, though it's not because I'm afraid of being overheard. The truth is, I'm so angry that I can hardly catch enough air to speak. "Bought for what?"

Her gaze meets mine and I see that she's smarter than I took her for. Her eyes are clear and intelligent. "Slaves," she says simply. "Sex or otherwise."

She slips away before I can ask her anything else and I watch her go, heart hammering. Auctions. High-end girls selling to the highest bidder. Forced to serve some man in their own home-town, where their families might see them. Where they can still see the streets they used to shop on. The homes they used to live in.

My God. I hadn't thought of it before. I knew we were going after human traffickers, but I hadn't really let that into my brain. It was just a label. Just the name of the people we were searching for. But now I'm forced to face it head on, and the prospect is horrifying. Girls whose lives are taken from them, and who are forced into something no human being should have to suffer. Forced to serve men they might have known in their previous life.

I've spent my whole life on the dark side of the law–hell, one of our casinos is just down the road, and I've killed more men in the back room of that casino than I can count, for cheating–but I've never felt as dirty as I do right now.

And not dirty in a good, playful sort of way.

I feel as though I've been doused in oil and then dusted with dirt that will never come off. I thought I was relatively jaded to the crime of life but this... I don't want this in my head. I want to bleach my brain of the knowledge.

And Brooks is in this ring.

My thoughts catch on that, and I suddenly wonder. An auction? They're auctioning the girls off? Does that mean they don't actually ship them anywhere? We were so sure there was an actual smuggling aspect to this, via ship, that we've been focusing on that over and above anything else, and I was sure we knew what we were doing.

But now I'm doubting myself. We don't actually have proof of any shipments. Just circumstantial evidence that we might have been forcing into our suspicions. Did we waste all that time at the docks, tracking ships, for an operation that only functions in the city? Do they only do auctions?

Has this been right in front of my face the entire time?

Once a week, that girl said, and the guard said the place is closed tonight. That must mean there's an auction happening.

The only auction this week. And we're within the window of a group of girls being shipped out. Or, as it happens, sold to the highest bidder.

If that timeline is true, and if our suspicions are correct, that means Aislyn's group should be on the block tonight. Literally.

And if they put Brooks in the same group, she'll be here, too.

If she's still alive. If she hasn't done anything stupid. The tracking device I gave her hasn't been working since they took her, and I don't know what to make of that. There's a chance the device just didn't work–it was a new version of tech–but there's also a chance they found it when they first kidnapped her. They would have been searching her for weapons, and if they had something that could pick up on tech embedded in a hair tie...

If they found it, they might have killed her for having something like that.

Devils, I could have gotten her killed by trying to protect her. Fuck, fuck, fuck. I turn and start pacing, willing my brain to come up with something useful. Why the fuck did I let her go in there without a plan to get her back out again? Why didn't I tell her she couldn't go?

Why the ever-loving fuck hadn't I done more to protect her?

Because you didn't think you had that right, a voice in my head says.

I close my eyes. The voice is right; I didn't think I had the right, at the time, because she told me I didn't. She flat out demanded that I stay out of her business and let her do what she was going to do, and because I'm an absolute idiot, I didn't push her on it.

I wanted to figure out what was going on, and she had the only good plan in the room. So I sat back and let it happen.

And now Brooks might be dead because of it.

Well, she doesn't get a say in the matter anymore, and that's all there is to it. She's not here. She doesn't get to tell me to stay out of her business. I've spent much of my life involved with that girl, and that has to count for something.

And I don't care if it doesn't. She's mine, and I'm not going to let some fucking trafficker sell her to another man.

"What's the move, boss?" Daniel asks suddenly, startling me out of my thoughts.

I open my eyes and look up at the dance hall. "We're coming back after dark. The place opens at 9. I want to be inside at 8. I need to know what the fuck is going on here. And get Brooks out before they try to sell her to some asshole politician."

And Satan help them if they'd already sold her.

Because I'll tear the city apart finding her again. And then I'd kill everyone who'd ever laid a hand on her.

***

T he thought is still with me hours later, when we creep through the darkness of an alley off Canal Street, looking for a way into the building. I brought several men with me, but none of my own. These are freelancers. Men outside the law who can't be tied back to me if they're found.

I still haven't told my father what I'm doing, and my own men being apprehended would get me into a world of trouble.

I go through the plan again, feeling off-balance without Daniel here. The man is a genius when it comes to brainstorming, and I almost always discuss plans out loud with him when we're on our way in, to make sure I haven't missed anything.

I feel as though I'm trying to walk with one fucking leg.

But I can't afford to lose him. If tonight goes wrong, I need him to keep searching for Brooks. We're so close to the end of our timeline that I can hardly stand it, and I'm keenly aware that I might lose her at any moment. She might have already left the city. I know the answer to that, of course; even if she has, I'll find her. I'll spend the rest of my life tracking her down if I have to.

The way I should have when she left New Orleans the first time.

That's unimportant at the moment, though, and I put it to the side. Right now, I'm going to break into this hall and find the closest office. If this is a hub for the ring and the location for auctions, then they'll have records here. All I need is a computer, and I'll be able to answer some questions. I need to know where else they're holding auctions and how often they happen. I need to know whether girls are also shipped out of the port, or if they sell here to buyers who then take them other places. Once I know where these auctions happen, I'll insert men into that circle and make sure they're invited to any auction. I don't know if I have the funds to purchase every girl and save her, but I need to know when they're happening so I can start figuring out who's running them.

I need to fucking find Brooks. Every single thing comes back to that, because the more I think about it the more I realize it's my fault she's in this position.

Sure, the girl is more stubborn than anyone I've ever met, and essentially told me what she was doing. But I let her go in there. I didn't argue with her, and I didn't pull her out of her father's house, shove her into a car, and take her home to hand-cuff her to my bed.

At the end of the day, it's my fault she's in New Orleans at all. I fucking brought her down here, promising that we'd find her friend, and instead she's fallen into their hands and I don't know how to get her back out again.

Correction.

I don't need to know how I'm going to do it.

I just need to know that I am. Because I'm not willing to fail. She's trusting me to come get her and I'll be well and truly fucked if I become just another man who's lied to her and let her down.

Suddenly I feel a change in the wall I'm creeping along, and I look down to find that I'm standing next to a door. Some sort of back exit to the hall, if I'm guessing. It's unmarked, though, and I hope that means it doesn't have an alarm attached to it.

I reach down and turn the handle, holding my breath against the potential of a siren going off.

There's nothing, though, and I breathe out in relief when the door opens like it's been waiting for me.

They left their back door unlocked. What are the fucking chances?

"Let's go," I tell the men behind me, pushing into the hallway and rushing forward. It looks like we're in some sort of basement, and if I know dance halls–I may have been in one or two–the main floor is where they'll hold the auction and the offices are on the upper floors. I locate the stairwell and push open the door, holding my breath again in case an alarm goes off.

Nothing.

These people must be extremely confident that no one is going to come in here and steal anything from them.

Idiots.

I run up three flights of stairs, not bothering to check on the men behind me, and then burst through the door into the main hallway. The first door I come to holds a desk with a computer, and that's all I need to see. I slide into the chair, turn the computer on, and wait. I'm not the best computer hacker I've ever met, but I'm decent.

Particularly when I'm fueled by absolute desperation.

"Come on, come on," I say, jittery with nerves. I want to get into this thing, find what I need, and get back out again before anyone discovers us.

When the computer finally starts up, it goes straight to the desktop.

They haven't protected it with a password.

Confident, indeed. I wonder briefly if they have security I don't know about–the cops? A security company?–and then decide I'll leave that up to the men I have in the hallway. My only job right now is research.

I dive into the files on the desktop and then search the hard drive, seeking anything that looks like it might be related to smuggling high-end girls. Or, as it turns out, selling them at local auctions. I find more information than I could have imagined, and start packing it into files, then zipping them up. One by one, I send them off to the email address Daniel created earlier today for this exact purpose. I have a thumb drive and am uploading everything quickly as I can, but we knew that might end up costing me too much time.

Emailing is faster.

And it answers the problem of me potentially losing the thumb drive.

Within ten minutes, I've got everything I can find and my internal clock is screaming, telling me every second that I don't have time to still be sitting here staring at a screen. I need to get the hell out of here before the person who actually works in this office shows up, or security discovers my men outside. I shut everything down, praying I got enough to tell us where Brooks is and stop the ring, and turn the computer off.

Now I have to get out of the building and around to the front, to enter as a potential bidder for the auction.

Yes, I've managed to secure an invitation. Don't ask me how much of my soul I had to sell to do it. If Brooks is being offered tonight, though, I'm not willing to stay away. I'll spend the rest of my soul, and the souls of everyone I know, to get her out of here.

I race into the hallway, motioning for my men to follow me,

but before I hit the stairs, my phone buzzes in my pocket. I take it out and see that Daniel is calling.

We don't have a call scheduled, which means this is important.

"What?" I hiss.

"Are you still in the building?" he asks, like he's just calling for a chat.

"Fucking yes. Did you actually need to call me to ask me that?"

"Get out of there. Don't stay for the auction. We know where she is."

I stop in my tracks. Brooks. They've found her.

"What?" I breathe.

"It's in the files you sent over. Brooks Landry, along with all her measurements."

Now my heart stops. "Where is she?" I whisper. "Is she still here? In the auction? What's going on?"

Daniel pauses for an eternity, and I'm ready to reach through the phone and choke him to death when he finally starts speaking again.

"She's not booked for the auction. I'm not sure how they decide which girls go to auction and which ones are shipped out, but they're running both routes through their operation. And Brooks is slated to be shipped out of the port. Tomorrow night."

My mind tears clean down the center at his words. Brooks isn't here, which means she's not about to be auctioned off to some NOLA asshole. She's safe for the night, but only until tomorrow.

I need to get home and make a new plan.

Which means I have to leave the girls here to their fates. They're probably downstairs already, maybe praying that someone will save them. But the girl I'm searching for isn't here, and if I'm going to save her, I need to figure out when she's shipping out and how I'm going to stop it.

Save the girls downstairs... or save Brooks.

I don't even have to think about it.

"We're on our way back to the mansion," I say, my feet racing down the stairs. "Get started on some planning. I want to have options when I arrive."

I feel horrible about leaving these girls behind, really I do. But let's be honest.

This was always going to be about Brooks. No one else matters.

19

BROOKS

It's official. I can't leave here without all these girls in tow. Even if I just met these ones.

Because Kate and I have now been separated from the group of girls I took the last couple of days getting to know. Gone is the blond who cries all the time and the one other redhead in the group, who looked like she might be willing to join in on any plan I came up with. Gone are the brunettes who all look so much the same, and the lone girl from Atlanta, who missed her sister so much she cried for her every night.

I worked for endless hours getting to know those girls and trying to bring them some comfort, and now they're all gone. Worst of all, I don't know what that means. When Kate and I were moved, the other girls were being 'tested' for how sellable they were. I glance across the memory of what that included—because no matter what they say, I'm a coward sometimes—and start trying to figure out what that means.

Were they taken right to a ship, to be sent out to other cities? Are they still sitting in that room being put through their paces?

Are they still alive?

I think they must be. This organization wouldn't go to all the trouble and expense of kidnapping so many girls just to kill them. It wouldn't make sense, and from what I've seen and heard, it would go against their standard MO. I still don't know what their goals are, but I've talked to enough of the girls to know they always follow the same pattern. They kidnap a certain number of girls any given week, and at the end of the week, they get rid of those girls. This mean there's a constantly revolving cast in any holding room, which I suppose makes it harder for girls to build alliances and plan for an escape. By the time they realize they need to escape, they've already been drugged and beaten up and have one foot out the door. Trying to plan anything has to be even harder for girls who aren't used to doing things for themselves in the first place.

And then I came along and disrupted everything. I've gotten to know some of the girls and have, against all the odds, found an old ally amongst the group. Together, we've been making some noise and I've even picked up some additional information.

Which is exactly how we find ourselves here, in a new building with a new group of girls.

I glance around, taking stock, and find that these ones are exactly the same as the others. Perhaps a little more worn around the edges, like they've been in the ring longer. Or maybe they've been hired out for a little extra cash. They look more tired, their skin paler, to the point that I wonder if they're sick.

And God, they're all so young.

The older part of me harps on that for a long moment. These girls need to go home to their mothers and be taken care of for two months, at least. They need the love and gentle hands of their own families, and instead they're about to be shipped to shores unknown to become slaves for terrible men.

I want to kill every one of those men with my bare hands. I want to kill the people running this smuggling ring.

But since neither of those things are possible, I'll settle for getting the girls the fuck out of here. I can come back and kill the men responsible for it after the girls are safe.

I look from them to the apartment around us, trying to figure out where we actually are. This one is a lot like the one we just came from, though: velvet on the walls, gold in the curtains, and lots of chaise lounges lying about the joint. Nothing useful. Nothing that tells me anything.

Except we're above ground, now, and I can hear the sounds of a city street outside. Cars on the road and the occasional horse-drawn carriage, which tells me we're in some sort of tourist neighborhood. Lots of shouting. Street vendors, though that's no different than many neighborhoods in the city, so it doesn't help me much.

Then I hear the sound of a trolley, and I freeze.

There's a trolley on the street outside, and that means a couple of things. The streetcar lines in the city serve as some of the most popular forms of public transportation, but they require a wire, just like trains require a track, and they can't exactly go off-roading.

They have to stick to the route they're given.

I listen closely, trying desperately to shut out the noises from within the room itself. If there's a trolley and it stops somewhere in this block, I should be able to hear–

"Does this one go out or in?" someone asks from right outside the window.

"Out," someone else answers.

Out or in. They're directions, because the trolley travels up and down this street, and if you get on it when it's going the wrong way, you'll be stuck for a while before you can get off and look for one going the other way.

Only one line goes out or in.

Canal Street. I'm on Canal Street. The guy at the last place said we were coming here, but I didn't know if he was lying, or if it was code for something else. But we're actually here.

We're actually here.

I almost break into tears, I'm so relieved. It feels as if it's been years since I knew where I was, and I'm giddy at the thought that right through that window, on the other side of this wall, is a street and neighborhood I know like the back of my hand.

Then I realize that this is the opportunity I've been waiting for, and it's back to business. I look around the room again and watch the guards for a moment. They're talking about the girls and something about bidding, but they haven't given us any details. And Kate and I are being left out of the preparation they're putting the girls through. Everyone else is dressed in slinky formal gowns, while we're still in the rough trousers and t-shirts they gave us at the last stop. I wonder if they're going to move the rest of the girls–and how long the doors are going to be open when they do.

I wonder if Kate and I can make a run for it.

Though that brings me back around to the thought that I'm not leaving here without those girls.

I skip that and progress with the plan. If I can get out of here and out onto the street, I can check the building for an address and then go find help. Once I have people on my side, I'll come back. Yes, that's what I'll do. I might have to leave the girls behind now, but I'll come back as soon as I find someone to help me break them out.

Who can I go to? Camille's no good. She may still be in my father's good graces, but she doesn't have any power of her own. My brother?

No. I'm not convinced he's on my side, and a large part of me still believes he might be involved in my father's activities.

And that leaves...

Lucien.

Who's the one person who's always been there when I needed someone, and stepped up to the plate. Damn him.

The problem is, of course, that I don't know if he's even still alive or whether he'll help me this time. He hasn't exactly broken down the door searching for me since I was picked up. Part of me knows it's unfair to think that, of course, and I've been through this one hundred times. The tracker in the hair tie must have stopped working, and without that, how the hell is he supposed to find me? We don't exactly have a way to communicate.

But being angry at him is better than believing he's dead, and that's the other option.

What if I can get all the girls out with me? Then I can hide them all and take more time finding someone to help me come back here and take down the men that kidnapped us. And then I don't have to leave the girls to fend for themselves. I like that plan better.

It's still not great, and there are a lot of things that could go wrong. I could really use some help.

I could really use a Lucien.

I also haven't yet found Aislyn. It would have been terrific if she was in this new group, waiting for me, but she's not here, either. The fact that I'm now in my second group–maybe third, if you count the girls who were in the first room in the catacombs–makes me think that there are many groups around the city. Aislyn must be in one of those. Unfortunately, I don't have addresses for any of their other outposts.

I have to admit that I'm starting to panic. My time is running out, both to find Aislyn and save myself. I have less than twenty-four hours until I think my timeline is up, and once I'm on a ship, I'm not going to have any escape route at all.

I have to get out of here. And I have to do it quickly.

Before I can dwell on that, another man enters the room. Not one of the guards. This one is dressed in some sort of matching shorts-and-shirt outfit that looks like it belongs on a child. The material is bright blue ombre, with a smattering of...

I stare, sure that I must be wrong.

Are those smiley faces?

They are. There are about a million bright yellow smiley faces spread over the blue background. His hair is slicked back, which just emphasizes the fact that he's going bald, and he's wearing sunglasses that went out of style twenty years ago.

What. The actual. Fuck.

He stops to speak to a guard and then looks at one of the girls, his expression full of curiosity. I follow his eyes and see one of the weepy blonds, and my body turns hot with rage. He's a buyer. He must be. The way he's fingering something in his pocket–a stack of cash?–and staring at the girl like he's looking at a porn magazine he wants to buy all make it obvious. I don't know why they've left him alone, but maybe this is how it works? They come in and pick the one they want, then the next buyer comes in?

I don't care.

I. Don't. Care.

He's not taking any of the girls I consider my wards.

I get up and walk toward him, taking in his height–he must be around 6'3"–and his weight. He's heavy, with some musculature but more fat, and I'm guessing he's dense but not nimble on his feet. Strong but not clever.

I don't know what I'm going to do with him until I do it. I pull up behind him and slip my hand from the middle of his back down to his ass. "You don't want her," I whisper in his ear, making my voice low and dusky. "She doesn't know what she's doing, yet."

He turns to me, half a smile on his lips, but frowns when he sees that I'm not dressed or made up like the other girls.

"What are you, the scullery maid?" he snorts. "You're not on the menu."

Oh my God I'm going to kill him. My body lights up with fire at his words and I barely manage to control my tone when I answer.

"I'm not for sale," I say with a shrug. "I take care of the men while they're making their choice."

I don't know what it means, but it sounds good, and the man seems to take it in stride. In fact, he suddenly looks a lot more interested in what I might be able to offer him.

"Take care of them?" he asks, his tone suggestive. "How do you do that?"

I lean even closer to him, repressing the need to gag at the body odor wafting off him. "I do whatever they want."

His grin grows as big as a Cheshire cat, and when I slip my hand into his and lead him away, he comes willingly. I've been watching the guards long enough to know the hallway outside the room will be empty right now, and I take the man out there, hoping for a bit of privacy.

He doesn't take long to flip me around, shove me against the wall, and try to shove his hand down my pants, his fingers sharp and grasping. I gasp, shocked and disgusted, and shove him backward. When he trips over his own feet, I take advantage of the movement and jump on his back, then practice my new favorite trick.

It's called Break a Man's Neck With Your Bare Hands. I wrap one hand around his cheek and brace the other on the opposite side of his neck, then jerk, using every ounce of strength in my shoulders and arms. I feel a very satisfying crunch and hear him gasp-slash-groan, and he goes limp, falling out from under me like he's a sack of potatoes.

I land on my feet and grin down at him, far too pleased at how easy that was. Then I realize that I'm standing in the hall with a dead body while men who think they have the right to sell me are in the next room.

"Stupid," I mutter.

I grab Blue Ombre Smiley Face Man under the arms and drag him quickly down the hall and around the corner, where I shove him into the first closet I come to. Then I go through his pockets for cash and weapons. He doesn't have weapons, but he does have a lot of cash.

And something even more important: a key card.

Once I'm done I slam the door on him, wishing him a speedy trip to hell, and run for the room we came from, trying like hell to remember where Kate was when I left.

Because I'll come back for the girls. But I'm not leaving Kate behind.

20

LUCIEN

The SUV jerked to a stop in front of yet another dance hall and I stared up at it, fury rolling off me. I didn't want to be here. I wanted to be at home making a plan for how we were going to get to Brooks tomorrow before she shipped out. But the moment I got back to the mansion, Daniel had come running out with more new information.

He'd hacked into the port's records and everything had been updated. The schedule we thought we knew was now gone, and nothing had replaced it. Currently, it looked like nothing was set to ship out at any time in the next week. Which was wrong, if we believed the records I downloaded at the first dance hall, and the timeline we thought we knew.

But without a confirmation for what time ships were leaving port tomorrow, we had no way of knowing where to look for Brooks. Or when to arrive. Hell, this had me doubting that they were going to ship girls out at all. Maybe they got wind of the fact that we were on their trail and were going to try to stop them, and decided to go a different direction.

In the end, we decided to go with the with one aspect we knew of: the auctions happening at the dance halls. We had a list of other halls involved, courtesy of that first set of data, and quickly decided on a new one so I wasn't returning to the scene of the crime. I already broke into the first dance hall, and if there were cameras in that building they'd be looking for me.

At a new one, they might know about me yet.

"You're sure this is the one you want?" Daniel asked from the driver's seat.

"Positive. You said they were taking Brooks to Canal Street, and this is the only other dance hall they have in this neighborhood."

Daniel huffs. "Are you here to figure out what's going on in this ring? Or just here for the girl?"

I grind my teeth together at the question, because he knows the answer just as well as I do.

"I'm here for Brooks," I snap. "The ring can wait."

"What about the other girls?"

Instead of answering, I shove the door open and get out of the car, checking my holsters for my knives and guns. I have everything but a plan, and that makes me nervous. I never do anything without a plan, and certainly nothing this big, but I don't see a way around it. As far as we know, the auction has already started here, and that means we don't have a lot of time to get in there and start searching. I need to get to another computer to see if the smugglers have updated their list of girls, and I need someone at the auction, making sure Brooks isn't one of the girls being sold off.

Yes, I'm here to stop the smuggling ring. I'll do whatever it takes to close this thing down.

But I want Brooks out of here first. And I'm not willing to be flexible on that point.

My men gather behind me, each of them armed and ready, and we run for the back of the hall. We're going in hot, but we still want to be hidden. If we can get in and out and get the information we need without them discovering us, that will be ideal.

We may be acting like the New York mafia right now, all blazing guns and flashy watches, but that doesn't mean I want to make as much noise as those New Yorkers do. I want to get in and get out, and then find my girl. I'm not willing to risk her for one more second. She's already been in this situation for too long, and I have no idea what's fucking happened to her since I last saw her. I'm caught between anger at her for going and anger at myself for letting her, and underneath all that is the simmering, long-standing frustration that I ever let her go in the first place. I should have chased after her when she left me, instead of being prideful and stubborn and bitter. I could have brought her home if I'd known what she was so upset about. I could have explained everything to her.

Instead, she moved to New York and found those lunatic friends, who taught her how to try to handle everything on her own. Brooks became that New York mafia. The loud, reckless ones who don't think anything bad can happen to them.

Which is how we find ourselves in this position. Another one of her stupid, dangerous ideas.

"Carlos, you go up front," I hiss as we run down the alley. "Get into that auction. Watch for Brooks. If you see her, bid on her. I don't care how much it costs. I'll pay the bill."

The man—one of my oldest and most loyal—doesn't ask questions. He peels off from the group and sprints back the way we came. I breathe out a bit at that. I trust the man, and know he'll do whatever it takes to keep Brooks safe. If she's here. If she's even in the auction rather than waiting to be shipped out.

The problem is I don't know.

I hate not knowing.

The rest of us sprint down the alley, looking for a door into the dance hall, and come to a stop when we find one. It looks the same as the door in the other building, and I wonder if all dance halls have the same basic layout. That would be extremely convenient.

So would finding this door unlocked.

It's not, but I learned how to pick locks when I was about five and wanted to be able to get into the pantry at all times of night. My father had found out about it and started locking the pantry, so I went to my uncle and asked him to teach me how to pick locks. He'd thought it was charming, as I was only five, and hadn't thought I had any plans to actually use the skill.

More fool, he.

The lock takes me about thirty seconds and then we're through the door and into the building. I don't know if all dance halls have the same layout, but this one is similar enough to the other for me to feel like I know exactly where I am. I look one way, then another, and then dash for the steps, taking them two at a time and heading for the third floor.

Behind me, I can hear Daniel on the phone, breathing hard as he listens to someone.

"Right," he finally says, and hangs up.

"What's going on?" I ask.

"Confirmation that there's an auction tonight," he says. "These girls were pulled especially for this event, and they're selling tonight rather than being shipped out to Russia or wherever they were going."

Selling tonight rather than shipping.

My gut tells me that includes Brooks, and that she's in this building somewhere, and every instinct I have is screaming for me to go find her. But I'm the best man on a computer, and I need information, too. Because if she's not here, then we still have to figure out where she is. And to do that, I need updated shipping manifests.

She'll be here. I'm positive she's here.

She's got to be. Because otherwise, I won't know how to find her. And I'm not going to lose her again.

I'll sell my soul to the devil before I let that happen.

21

BROOKS

I manage to stop running moments before I get to the door of the room where they're keeping the other girls, and walk in like I didn't just hide a dead body in a closet.

Unfortunately, my absence hasn't gone unnoticed.

"Where have you been?" a guard snarls, hurling me against the wall.

I grunt when my head hits the wall behind me, but don't let it slow me down. I don't have time to stand around talking to this asshole. Please see what I said above about leaving a dead body in a closet.

I'm pretty sure these guys are going to be pissed when they realize what I did.

"Bathroom," I gasp. "I had to pee." I open one eye and glare at the man in front of me. "Actually, as long as I have your attention, what the fuck is going on here? How long are you going to hold me? Because I have a date tomorrow night and I need to get my hair done before I go."

He freezes, the way I knew he would, and then practically runs away from me. They always do that when I ask too many questions, like they're afraid I'm somehow going to kill them with any knowledge they give me.

I mean, I might.

I smile after him, then turn and continue into the girls' room. I need to get Kate, and we need to get the fuck out of here.

She's across the room when I enter, talking to one of the girls, and I motion for her to dump the girl and get into the corner where we have the most privacy. I've been watching the guards since we got here, and at this point I can guess here they're going to be and when. That includes knowing that they never come near the corner I'm now in.

Handy, when you're trying to foment rebellion and need to meet with your lieutenant.

"What's going on?" Kate asks when she arrives. "And why do you look..."

She gestures vaguely at my face and I lift one eyebrow, waiting for her to get to the point.

"Like you just went into the hallway and took heroin or something," she finishes.

I frown. "What the fuck does a person look like after they take heroin?"

"I don't know, flustered and worked up. Go look in the mirror and you'll get a good idea. Were you out there taking drugs?"

"Yeah, I found some in the hallway and figured I'd try them out," I say, almost laughing. "That's what every good rebellion needs, isn't it? People too high to know what they're doing. No, I wasn't doing drugs, but we've got trouble."

Her face turns immediately more serious. "What kind of trouble? What actually happened out there?"

"Short version? I saw a buyer bothering one of the girls and took him off her hands. Then I killed him and shoved him in a closet."

I have never seen Kate at a loss for words, but she opens her mouth and then closes it again, like she doesn't have any language available to her. She stares at me for one beat, then two, before she finally finds something to say.

"You killed him and shoved him in a closet. Right. I guess that means it's time to get out of here."

"So glad you agree with me," I hiss. I grab her arm and tow her toward the door of the room. "I don't know how long it'll take them to figure out what happened, but I'd rather not be here when they do. It's time for us to make our escape."

She snorts, now. "You think they're just going to let us walk out?"

We get to the door and out into the hall, and I guide her so we're walking close to the wall. "That's exactly what I think. I've been watching their routes and they've only got one guy on duty right now. I already scared him off by asking too many questions. We should have an open pathway down to the front door."

"And how are we going to get through it?" she responds, falling into stride next to me and matching her steps to mine. "Because they're idiots if they don't have a lock on that door."

I fish the key card I stole from Smiley Face Man out of my bra and flash it at her, grinning widely. "That's where the key comes in handy."

She looks like I just told her we could eat all the candy in the world, her eyes going big and glassy with excitement. "Where the fuck did you get that?"

I shrug. "The guy I killed had it in his pocket. Got some cash, too. Figure we might need a ride when we get out."

She chuckles but doesn't ask any more questions, and we stride down the hall, doing our best to look like we belong out here and like we're definitely not trying to escape with a key card I stole off the guy I killed and then hid in a closet.

***

By the time we get downstairs to the foyer, I've come up with a pretty solid plan. We're going to get out of the building and onto Canal Street. I know the area well and can see that we're in a dance hall, which puts us in the entertainment district. Boudreaux will have gambling halls just down the street. We'll get to one of them and demand to see Lucien. If he's not there, I'll tell whoever I find to call him. Once he arrives, we'll come back for the girls. Then we'll hit every other dance hall on the street and save the girls there, too.

When they're safe, we can talk about taking down my father and whoever he's working with. My father isn't the man in charge, I don't think—he's not important enough to be running this whole thing himself—but he's got to know the head guy. And my fingers are itching to start torturing him for information. He's working for someone bigger, and if my suspicions are correct, we'll save hundreds of girls when we take them down. Maybe thousands. The girls in New Orleans. The ones from Atlanta and Boston.

Aislyn.

Bonus: If this works, I'll never have to worry about my father again. Because I plan to make sure he's behind bars for the rest of his life. Or dead.

I just have to pray that Lucien's willing to help me out one more time.

Pray that he's still alive. Because somewhere, deep down in my stomach, a fear has been growing. I've never known that man to give up on anything he wanted. If he has his mind set on something, he'll move heaven and hell to get it. Sell his very own soul, and the souls of all his family members. I don't like that he hasn't found me yet.

It reminds me of when he didn't come find me in New York, and makes me wonder if he's decided he's had enough of me.

Or if he's dead.

That thought scares me enough that I haven't been willing to touch it, and even now I shy away from looking at it too closely. I can't imagine a world without Lucien in it. It's been years since we were together and I'm not entirely sure how I feel about him, but he's one of those forces of nature that keeps the world running. He's the one I instinctively each for when I'm in trouble.

The only person who really knows me. And the only one who's never let me down.

I don't want to live in a world without him, and the realization is a shocking one.

Because what if he's out there dead because he tried to save me from this stupid, stupid plan that we never even discussed?

I'm jerked out of the thought by a guard, who comes around the corner ahead of us, spots me, and lunges forward. Kate sees him coming before I do and manages to get out of the way, but I'm a step too slow.

"You!" he snarls, grabbing me and throwing me against the wall.

"Me," I agree, gasping at the impact. I drag my eyes up to meet his, knowing I look like I'm about to murder him.

I don't care. I don't know what the fuck this guy is, but he's getting in the way of us getting out of here, and that means he's on borrowed time.

"You're not supposed to be down here."

That's true, but also doesn't require an answer, and I can see by his face that he doesn't realize what's actually going on. He doesn't think we're trying to escape.

He thinks we're just lost or something.

I seal my lips shut and stare at him, waiting for him to continue. And because I've found that when you stare at someone, it makes them intensely uncomfortable. They forget what they were so upset about and focus on wondering why the hell you're staring at them.

He does just that, blushing and getting flustered, and I almost laugh at how well it works. He draws back a step, like he's just going to let us keep going, and I start coming up with the script we'll need to get out of this. Just tell him we got lost. Keep going. Get the fuck out of here without anyone suspecting anything. Leave this guy to answer for why he didn't stop us when he had the chance.

Then he yanks out his gun and holds it to my head, and I realize that's not going to work.

"Get back upstairs and stop playing your tricks, girl. The boss has special plans for you," he snarls.

Shit. So much for taking the easy way.

And him pulling a gun on me already is a problem I didn't see coming.

My mind flies through several different options, cataloging every possibility, but I'm not sure I can pull any of them off, and panic starts to rush through my veins. I don't have anything but a card key and a stack of cash, and neither of those is going to get this guy off me. Even worse, I don't know if he has orders to shoot. He might pull that trigger the moment I start to move.

I'm in trouble.

I'm about to move anyhow, counting on my instincts to be faster than this guy's, when he clicks the safety off.

"Don't even think about it," he mutters.

Christ. Even I can tell this is bad. He's just caught me trying to escape—and failing—and if he takes me back up to that room things are going to get ugly. This is my chance, and this asshole has me pinned against a wall, ready to shoot me.

Shit, shit shit. How do I get out of this? *Think, Brooks, think!*

And then someone else speaks.

"She's mine. Let her go."

The world stops spinning, because I know that voice.

Lucien.

Lucien is here.

22

LUCIEN

The man doesn't move, just stands there like a fucking idiot with his gun still pressed to Brooks' head, his eyes on her and his knuckles white with how hard he's clutching that gun.

Drop. The. Gun," I grind out. I want to kill the cunt. Rip him apart with my own hands for daring to threaten her. But I'm going to give him one chance to save his own life.

I know he won't drop it.

I know it won't matter if he does.

Because I've been searching for Brooks for what feels like years now, and this man is the only thing standing between me and her. It's the most dangerous place in the world to be, and he's going to pay for it.

He doesn't drop the gun.

So I shoot him in the head.

He drops to the ground and I kick him aside, my eyes on my girl and my hands already reaching for her. She's covered in blood now from the guy I just killed and she looks thinner than the last time. Shadows under her eyes, and her hair is a rat's nest of tangles and curls. I could make a joke about how she looks and the fact that she probably needs a shower. I could say a lot of things.

But she's never looked more glorious, and for a long moment the world around us slows down and fades into nothing more than background noise. I lift my hand up and run my fingers gently down her cheek, over her jaw, and to her neck. With my other hand I touch her lips, her nose, her eyelids. Brush a thumb across those eyebrows that are constantly telling me exactly what she's thinking. I dust the skin of her cheeks with my own skin, trying to convince myself that she's real and here. Not sold to some other man or awaiting shipment. Not dead or left in a ditch or deserted in some place where I can't get here.

Something is happening inside me that I don't understand. I feel as though someone has put a balloon inside me and decide to inflate it too quickly. The feelings are growing, expanding until I think I'm going to explode, and I don't understand any of it. Two weeks ago, I barely remembered that Brooks was ever a part of my life, and now I don't feel like I can breathe unless I know she's safe and happy.

It's the stupidest possible thing to want from a girl who lives a reckless, dangerous life and never does what anyone else tells her to.

And yet.

I'm about to kiss her, bury myself in her and mark her as my own, scream at her for leaving me and being so stupid, when a voice suddenly breaks through the bubble I've built around us.

"And here I thought you two were just friends."

I turn, confused because I thought I just shot the only other person in this hallway, and find a face I never expected too see.

"Kate Fontenot?"

Brooks grabs my arm and the world starts moving again, and I realize there's smoke and screaming all around us, chaos personified while I'm standing here making up fucking poems about Brooks Landry.

"Yeah, it's a long story," she snaps. "And we've got to get the hell out of here. I killed someone upstairs and the guards are coming for me."

We're running before I know what we're doing, and two thoughts are racing through my brain.

One: Of course she killed someone.

Two: That's my fucking girl, and I wouldn't expect anything less. And now I'm going to get her home and remind her exactly who she belongs to—and that I'll kill her if she ever does anything like this again.

My final thought as I race through the door, though, is that she will. And I'll have to save her again. And I'll show up for her, just like I always have.

Just like I always will.

23

BROOKS

I'm surprised when we don't return to his mansion, and go instead to an apartment above an old jazz club in Tremé.

"Why are we here?" I ask, looking around the place. It's well-appointed, done in rich leather and deep reds and greens, and looks like a place an old man would keep for the weekends. Lots of furniture and views of the city outside make my think that this is actually someone's home.

Wait, *is* this someone else's home?

Does Lucien keep another apartment in the city, for when he can't make it home? Camille told me that he went through a phase of dating every girl in the city, and suddenly I wonder if he keeps an apartment for his girls to sleep at. Maybe he actually keeps a girl here and she's about to come out of the bathroom or something.

Look, I'm not normally a jealous person, but the thought of him having a girl on the side makes me want to murder someone. I've spent days obsessing about where he was and whether he was dead, and it's allowed something to grow inside me that I wasn't expecting.

Something that feels a lot like possessiveness.

Of a man I can't actually claim as my own.

I've barely finished the thought before Lucien comes in behind me, grabs me, and spins me to face him. His arms go around my waist and yank me against his body, and he's hotter than any human being should be. He's burning up, like someone lit him on fire before he entered the apartment, and the heat passes through me until I feel the fire licking through my veins, as well. The flames rush into my face and then southward, where they pools between my legs, the surge of lust making me feel as though my bones are melting, my body becoming fluid in his arms like it's trying to merge with his.

"Stop thinking this is an apartment I keep for other girls," he whispers against my mouth.

"I wasn't thinking that," I say, though my voice is weak and unconvincing.

His eyes drop to my lips and a smile curves the corners of his mouth. "Yes you were. Your poker face isn't as good as you think it is, Brooks Landry."

"Stop calling me that," I protest. "That's not my name anymore."

He kisses me slowly, like we have all the time in the world and he's going to savor me for hours. His lips are soft and insistent, but so gentle I feel as if I could cry, and I open up beneath him like a flower that's finally seen the sun. Sparks explode through my body and the butterflies I've been keeping at bay rise up in my lower stomach, singing like they've been waiting years for this.

The truth is, they have.

His tongue sweeps into my mouth as his hands go to my hair, pulling it sharply to tip my head up to his. I don't fight it. I'm too busy reveling in having his hands on me again. His lips on mine and his body pressed up against me. He's hard and ready, his erection a rod against my belly, and I'm melting for him. I want our clothes off and a bed right now. I don't think I can stand another moment without him inside me. His skin naked against mine.

His whispers on my skin as he fucks me.

He pulls away, though, his eyes teasing with that laughter I used to love so much.

"You'll always be Brooks Landry to me," he whispers. Then he tugs on a lock of hair. "Just like I'll always expect you to be blond. I've known you too long to think of you as anything different."

The statement hits me in a way I don't expect, with the blunt reminder that this man is part of my history. In a world where I've had to build a whole new life with people who don't know who I really am, Lucien's a rock. A foundational part of me. He's seen all of me, knows the things that built me into who I am.

And that means more than I ever thought it would.

"I'm never going back to blond," I say, needing to fight him on *something*.

His smirk turns into a grin. "I didn't say I mind the red. I kind of like it. Matches your personality. Go have a shower. You smell like other men, and I don't like it."

He turns me and shoves me toward the hallway, and I allow myself a secret grin of my own.

I like that he doesn't like me smelling like other men.

Though I'm not going to look too closely at the reason for that. If I did, I'd have to admit that I might be catching feelings for him. And that is something I can't afford.

***

B y the time I get out of the shower, the apartment has changed from lazy, leather-clad luxury to a war room. The walls are covered with maps and lists, laptops clutter the dining room table, and Lucien has brought in not only Daniel Boniface, but Camille and a few men I don't recognize.

"What's going on?" I ask, forcing my mind to kick into gear.

If we're planning war, I want in. I hate that I've left so many girls behind, and I still don't know where Aislyn is or how we're going to get her out.

As far as I'm concerned, I may have escaped but my job isn't done yet. Far from it.

Lucien looks up from where he's bent over the table, running his finger over a map. "We've had news from the inside of the ring. The auctions tonight were disrupted by the cops and the smugglers have changed their schedules. They've arranged for more ships than they originally planned, to get rid of the girls that should have gone to auction. The cops have the girls they seized, but that doesn't account for all of them. And once they're on those ships…"

"Once they're on the ships, we lose them," I say, moving toward him. "So we need to know the names of the ships and when they're leaving. Then find a way to stop them."

He smiles a wry, resigned sort of smile. "Exactly."

I start looking at what they've got and immediately see the problem. Manifest after manifest lines the table, but they're not going to tell us anything. All the ships leaving the New Orleans port are listed on here. Small fishing boats. Large cruise ships. Personal yachts and sailboats and speedboats, taking rich people out for the day or week. There are plenty of shipping vessels, but we don't have their cargo lists, and even if we did, it we wouldn't know what they meant.

Smuggling vessels don't exactly list their true cargo, particularly when they're transporting human girls.

"We know the original ship though," I say, remembering what I already know. "The first one. The one that would have..." My voice drops off when I'm unwilling to finish the sentence.

"Would have carried you, yes," he says, filling in the gap. "But we don't know what the rest of the ships are named, or when they're leaving, and I'm worried that the girls who should have been auctioned tonight have already reached their expiration date. The smugglers might not take much time to get them on another ship. Surely they have lists of ships to use in case of emergency."

I swallow hard at that one. I don't know the girls who were going to auction tonight very well, but that doesn't change how much I want to save them. Every single girl in that ring deserves a better chance.

And every single man involved deserves to have his balls cut off and shoved down his throat.

I narrow my eyes, then, catching on two things that don't make sense. I was so intent on figuring out where we are that I didn't process them at first.

"Wait. How do you know the auctions were interrupted? Did you leave men there to keep an eye on things?"

He shrugs, but I can see the pride in his face. "I told the cops what was happening. The smugglers had paid them well to stay away, and thought they were protected. Those idiots thought they were safe. They never saw it coming."

Well that doesn't make sense. "And the cops raided them even after they were paid not to?"

He goes back to looking at the maps in front of him. "I paid them better. I want those girls safe, and we can't save them if they're with fifty different men. I'd rather they all be in one place."

I stop for a moment, stunned at how casually he's become a hero, but then carry on. "And how do you know they've decided to ship them out?"

"I have a man on the inside."

This is so surprising that I actually do a double take. "You have what? Since when? How? Who?"

"Simon leBanc. Since about two days ago, though this is the first time he's given me anything of real value. Well. The second, if you include the manager he turned over to me for... questioning."

My mind is reeling with all this new information, but I stick on one particular point. "Simon leBanc? The outlaw? You know you can't trust him." I might not know much about New Orleans anymore, but I remember Simon from my time here before.

He doesn't belong to any family and has never been anyone's friend. Not really. I thought Lucien had better taste than that.

He looks up and meets my eyes again. "Hence the maps and lists in front of you, love. He's not important enough to have any good information, though. He's given us broad strokes with no details. I believe him when he says the smugglers have decided to ship the girls rather than auctioning them, and I believe him when he says he doesn't know any more than that. So we have to figure out where they're sending them, and how, so we can stop it before it happens."

"In that case, I think I can help," I tell him.

His eyes narrow. "I'm counting on it. What do you have?"

"I've been in their computer system, and I know the names of the girls they're shipping. Plus the codes for the ships. I don't have them written down, but I do have something even better."

He takes this in like I've just given him the recipe for my grandma's corn bread, and I want to punch him. But he doesn't know what I do about what I've been up to.

I didn't go undercover for my own fucking health.

"I've also got this." I slide the card key across the table and watch it land right in front of him, then look up with a triumphant smile. "It'll get you into the dance hall where they were keeping me. I'm guessing they're not there right now. Seeing as how they were just raided."

He looks up at me, and now his face is showing the proper amount of surprise. "You have a key to their building? How the fuck did you get that?"

Now it's my turn to shrug and grin like I know exactly what I'm doing. "I did some lifting while I was there. You need information? Then let's go get it."

He pauses for a beat, no doubt reorganizing his plans, and then nods once. "You know we're going to start a war with your family over this. If your father is running this ring, or even cooperating, this is going to end him."

I snatch a croissant from the tray sitting next to me and take a bite. Because if we're about to go to war, I want to have a full stomach.

"Good," I say. "I've been wanting to take that asshole out since I was thirteen. It just took me a while to figure out how to do it."

24

LUCIEN

I glare at the men sitting around the table, furious that they're taking so long to decide. This isn't rocket science. I'm going after a smuggling ring and I need backup. It's not that I need the men–I don't–but I want to know that once I start this war, I'll have support in the city to finish it.

It's not a question of not starting the war, either. Brooks wants it, and I'm not going to be the one to tell her no. She'd probably kill me if I did.

And these men should be on my side about that. Crow Lafayette runs in some of the same rackets as Boudreaux, so we've had deals with each other before. I don't call a lot of people friend, but Crow is as close as it gets in my world. If I were in trouble and none of my own men were available, I'd go to Crow and expect him to at least hear me out.

Jonathan Benoit isn't technically in the underworld anymore. He took his family up into the light several years ago, and they're legitimate business people now. But he's still got interest in the shipping industry, and I went to him first to see if he could help me stop ships from leaving the docks.

He hasn't answered me yet.

As for Sean Duhon...

He's the only man in this meeting I'd call a cold-blooded killer. He's as crooked as they come, and has more power in this town than almost anyone else. He's got his fingers in everything. Gambling, entertainment, shipping, gun running, drugs, politics, and girls. I don't like the man. Honestly, I usually go out of my way to avoid him. But he knows about the meat trade and if anyone has an inside route to figuring out who's running this ring, it's him. Being in the same room as him leaves a very bad taste in my mouth, but if it means we knock this ring down and take Dom Landry out, I'm willing to do it.

Now that I have Brooks safely at home, I want to save the girls she's after. I want to help her find Aislyn. And if that means dealing with people who make me want to bleach my own eyes afterward, I'll do it.

For her.

The other thing about these three men is that they all hate the Landry clan almost as much as I do. Dom has made enemies of them all, either through business or through his sparkling personality, and I thought that if I brought them here and told them I had a way to take him down, they'd jump at the possibility.

So far, none of them is jumping.

And I don't have the fucking time to sit around and wait for them to make up their minds. I need to get to the dance hall and use Brooks' card key to get into their offices again. Figure out if I missed anything, and then rectify it. We need to know when the smuggling ships are leaving and what they're called, then get to the port ahead of their departure times and stop them.

"He's going to get caught, at some point," I say quietly. "And before he does, he'll wreak havoc on the city. He's going to have the FBI on his ass, for sure, and maybe DHS. None of us wants that. This isn't just a Boudreaux war. It's a war to keep our city clean."

Sean Duhon chuckles at that, and I flash him a reluctant smile.

"Yes, I know, the wording is... ironic. But you know what I mean. None of us needs the feds down here."

The three men murmur amongst themselves, and I know I'm getting to them. They hate Dom enough to want to take him down, but the bigger motivation is that they don't want the FBI in town. New Orleans exists somewhat outside of the law, thanks to our lack of organization when it comes to crime, and we like it that way.

If Dom causes enough trouble, though, the law dogs are going to start looking at us too closely.

But if we can take him down, we get rid of Dominick Landry and close down a ring that might bring the feds to our doorstep. We prove to the feds that we're still maintaining a clean city, or something like it. We don't give them an excuse to look twice at us. It's a win-win.

And a triple win for me, because I have the added benefit of laying this gift at Brooks' feet. It's not just that I want to help her take her father out. It's that I want to make sure she never has to deal with him again. Give her the vengeance she's searching for, for what he did to her when she was a kid.

Make the city safer.

Because I can't bring her home until it's safe for her to be here. And that will never happen if Dominick Landry is still here, and especially not if he's controlling a smuggling ring that's disappearing girls right and left. If I can take him down, and make sure he doesn't come back, then I can give her the safety she's never known, and always wanted.

She might not admit it, but this is what she's been searching for her whole life.

And I'm the man to give it to her.

I just need some of my contacts to help me make sure it sticks.

Do I wish I could do it all on my own? Absolutely. Do I want to go straight to her, drop to my knees, and beg her to stay here and let me take care of her? Yes. But I'm not a hero. I'm not a good guy. I'm as crooked as they come, as shifty as necessary to get things done, and I'll pull the shiftiest, most crooked deal I've ever cooked up if it means she's safe.

It doesn't have anything to do with the Boudreaux family or the promise I made to my father. Not anymore.

This time, it's only about Brooks and the partnership I think we could have together.

"We need some time to think about what you're saying," Jonathan finally says, his black eyes expressionless.

Asshole.

I stand up, ready to move on to the next task, and look at each of them in turn. "Fair enough. I'm going to stop this ring with or without you, gentlemen. The war starts tonight, and I'll count on you to join me tomorrow. You can take your time making your decision. But when it comes to dividing up the power that's left after Landry falls, don't expect me to count you in unless you've done your part."

I turn and walk away, cane swinging and mind flying forward to the next thing on my list. We have six hours until we know one of the ships is leaving. I need to get home and check on my crew, then head to the dance hall and break into their computers to collect any new information. I need to somehow convince Brooks to stay at home where it's safe.

And I need to gather my men and get ready to go to war.

***

When I arrive home, however, my plans change. Because the moment I pull into the driveway, Camille comes running out, her face a mask of horror.

I get out of the car so quickly I nearly trip.

"What the fuck are you doing here?"

"Brooks called me over to help her with some research," she says breathlessly. "We were working on figuring out whether there were any codes in the shipping manifests we had when she suddenly stopped and started laughing. She said she had to go to the bathroom and left. An hour later, when I finally went searching for her, I found this."

She hands me a piece of paper and I don't know if I even have the stomach to look at it.

Because I know Brooks better than anyone else in this world, and my instincts have already told me what I'm going to see written there. The girl is stubborn and reckless and dangerous, and she's entirely too sure of her own importance in the world. Every idea she has is a bad one, but she always manages to luck out of getting into trouble.

And the more she succeeds, the more invincible she thinks she is.

I look down at the sheet of paper, and I'm not surprised by what it says.

"If I don't make it, tell him I tried," I murmur.

I stand there for a moment, mind blank and heart hammering, and then I crush the paper in my hand and make for the house. I thought we had until tonight before we went for the port.

But Brooks just changed the timeline, because she can't fucking sit still.

And this time, I'm not going to let her go in there alone.

25

LUCIEN

Generally I go into any situation with a plan, and a backup to that, and a backup to that. I like to know what I'm getting into and how I'm going to get out of it, and I always have people who are better than the people we're going up against.

I go into any battle expecting to win, and I set myself up for that victory every time.

But tonight I'm going in hot and reckless and out of control, and I don't even care that it's a stupid fucking idea. I got that note from Brooks and knew that I didn't have a second more to waste, because she's done something stupid that is inevitably going to get her into trouble.

And like always, I'm here to fucking make sure she gets out alive again. Because I'm no hero–I'm the devil in the dark who's always trying to trick you into doing something dumb–but when it comes to Brooks, I always end up playing some kind of stupid fucking white knight, riding in on my charger to save the day she's trying to blow up with a hand grenade she got from some shady guy in a back alley.

I have never met anyone who tries harder to get themselves

killed, and then calls it badass and convinces herself she's immortal.

And fucking hell do I love the girl. I don't think I ever realized how much before, but this has been growing in my belly since she disappeared from her father's house, and at this point I'm finished lying to myself about it. The sheer panic of knowing she may have gone in again, and the bigger frenzy of realizing I don't know how to get her back out again, is forcing me to admit the truth.

I love Brooks Landry.

Fuck, I've loved her for a very long time. I've just spent the last ten years pretending it wasn't true, because loving her and losing her was too much for my ego to take.

But I'll be damned if I'm going to lose her again. This time, when I find her, I'm tying her up and handcuffing her to my bed. I'm going to force her to marry me and then I'm going to tell her she's never allowed to come up with any stupid plans again unless they involve sexy lingerie and her being in my bed.

I growl at the thought and throw open the door the moment the SUV stops, then gather my men and start going over what we do know.

"We only know about the one ship, so that's the one we're after," I say firmly, looking each of the men in the eye. "I'm not sure whether they've involved other ships, but we can't worry about that right now. The other girls are going to have to wait a second. Brooks knows what we know, which means she'll be going after the ship we already have in our targets. We find her and we get her the hell out of here. Then we start working on how to take down their organization."

No one responds to that, so I keep going.

"They have to get the girls here somehow. I'm guessing a truck drives right to the loading dock. But there'll be at least ten minutes where they're moving the girls from the truck to the ship. That's when we're going to make our move."

Every man nods as if this is no big deal, and I feel a moment of pure love for them. Some of these guys have known Brooks since we were all kids, and some of them just met her. But they're all willing to lay their lives on the line to rescue her, and that tells me everything about them.

These are good men.

And they're going to help me make sure we get her home.

"We get in there, rescue the girls, and get everyone back out again. Get them to safety. No girl left behind. Hard stop."

More nodding. No arguments.

I turn and look out over the water, trying to decide if there's anything else. But there's not. We know everything we're going to know, and we're the only ones showing up for these girls. I wish we had a better plan and more backup, but there's no time for that now.

Every second that passes is a moment too long. Every second is one where those men could be hurting Brooks.

I glance at my watch and see that we have half an hour until we expect the trucks to arrive. We need to find the ship and find cover. I want the element of surprise when they arrive. If we're lucky, we'll be able to pick the guards off from afar, then rescue the girls without having to defend them from violent men.

I hope to God Brooks is with the group of girls we're going after. I don't know what, exactly, she has in mind–her note was light on details–but this is the only thing I can think of, and it makes sense that she would go back in.

After all, the best way to take an organization down is by infiltrating it.

Her father taught her that the day he tried to send her into the Boudreaux family as a mole.

And now, if I know Brooks, she's trying to use what he taught her to send him to jail.

Devils, I love that girl.

"Let's go," I growl.

We take off into the night on foot, our eyes on the containers in the distance and our hands on our guns as we seek the ship that's going to try to steal my girl away from me.

* * *

By the time we get to where the containers are stored, I'm starting to get suspicious. Everything in the port is quiet. The ships are at anchor and the containers are deserted. This place should be crawling with workers, and instead it's a fucking ghost town.

What the fuck is going on here? Where are the dock and ship workers? Where's all the noise that usually comes with the port, and where the fuck are the trucks that should be carrying the girls for the ship?

I look to the left and let my gaze run along the ships in their births, looking for the name of the ship we've targeted. It's sitting right there, lights off and looking like it's parked for the long haul. That's not a ship that's getting ready to head out. That's a ship that doesn't have a date with the open water tonight.

And suddenly I remember my earlier fear that the idea of this ship was a bait and switch. Hell, they've already thrown additional complications into the picture with those fucking auctions, and then canceling the auctions and deciding to ship all the girls out instead. These people evidently don't believe in plans either, and like to change their direction at the drop of a hat.

What if something else has changed and they're not even here? What if they aren't coming, and we've just rolled out for no reason?

What if they have Brooks and they're taking her out of the

city by train right now, while I'm fucking around at the docks? If someone tipped Dominick off that they had her again...

Oh my God, what if they took her right to him, and he has her right now?

That's almost more terrifying than anything else. If a buyer has her, I'll track her and get her back. I'll pay whatever I have to pay to save her. But if Dominick has her and knows she was trying to take his operation down...

He did enough damage to her when he claimed to love her, and when she was nothing more than a child.

I can't imagine what he'll do to her if he knows what she's been up to.

I pull out my phone and dial Simon's number, desperate for news.

"Boudreaux," he says by way of greeting.

"We're at the docks and they're quiet," I say without preamble. "There's supposed to be a load going out tonight. What the fuck is going on?"

He snorts. "There's still a load going out tonight. Dock workers just know to stay out of their way when they're loading the girls. What you're seeing is the product of a lot of money changing hands, my friend."

"They're here?" I hiss. "Are you sure?"

"Dead positive."

I hang up without answering, and look to my men. "Simon says they're here somewhere. That's the ship they're going to be loading. Let's make enough noise to draw them out."

We go in screaming like banshees, our guns blazing and our knives swinging, like there's actually someone in there to fight, and to my surprise, it works.

Men appear from out of nowhere, shooting and shouting, and behind them, I see a row of vans I didn't see before, their windows dark and their doors opening. Girls are already running out of the vans, guards at their sides dragging them toward the ship. Those are the girls, I realize. They're already loading, and we haven't killed the guards yet. Fuck, we wouldn't have even seen them if we didn't decide to attack ahead of time, and now we're a step behind and everything is going sideways.

Well, when it comes to catching up, there's no time like the present.

I start picking off the guards, rushing toward them like a fucking madman, and I can see that they're confused by our behavior. This isn't what any self-respecting New Orleans gangster does. Down here, we're more subtle. We rely on trickery over outright warfare.

But I'm not just a gangster. I'm a pirate, and it turns out I've learned something from my new friends in New York.

We go in screaming, and beneath my scream, hiding in plain sight, is fury that these men have dared to touch my girl and steal her again. I feel possessed, like a man who has actually made a deal with the devil. Except I didn't get any guarantee that I'd get my girl back when I sold my soul.

At this point, I'm flying blind, and I hate that.

When I see Brooks in the line of girls, her flaming hair lighting up the night around her and her eyes big in her face, my anger reaches a whole new level. I shoot and kick and slice, going through men like they're smoke, my eyes on the girl in the distance. She stops the whole line and stares at me, her mouth open like she's shouting something, and I have enough time to wonder why the fuck she thinks this is the time for a conversation before she's hidden by the raging battle around us.

I slice through the man in front of me and shoot one running for me, swerve and spin to avoid someone's knife, and come up shooting again. I get rid of the spent magazine and reload my gun on the run, my eyes on the place where I last saw Brooks.

When the space clears, though, she's gone.

And when I look for the line of girls, she's no longer with them.

I scream, furious, and shoot man after man to get to the spot where she was. When all the guards in our area are dead, I turn to my men.

"Follow the girls!" I shout. "Save the guards for questioning! I'm going to find Brooks."

I run through the containers, taking turn after turn and shouting for her. No matter how many alleys I take, though, I can't find her, and I'm starting to think I need to slow down and actually come up with a plan when I see something on the ground. The sky above is dark but I'm standing under an old light meant to make it easier to find the container you're looking for, and in the faded yellow light of the lamp I see...

Blood on the ground.

A trail of blood on the ground.

I gasp and run to it, bending down to dip my fingers into it.

This blood is still warm. Someone's bleeding. And if the trail is correct, they went into a container across the alley from me.

Heart in my mouth with fear, I rush to the container and throw it open, terrified that someone was hit in the gunfight. I'm even more worried that Brooks herself did something she shouldn't do, and managed to get herself hurt.

Or killed.

When the door opens, I find Brooks sitting near the entrance, bleeding from the head, another girl in her lap, and though my heart leaps at the idea that she's still upright, one look at her wound tells me she won't be in the position for long.

And the girl in her lap looks like she might already be dead.

26

BROOKS

They say when you're dying, your life flashes before your eyes.

All the things you've ever done or seen or said. The places you've been. The thoughts you've thought.

The people you've loved.

They also say that this is actually your brain going through your entire bank of knowledge and experience, trying to find a way to keep your body alive. I've always thought that's kind of terrible. Your body is dying and your brain–still very much alive and wanting to stay that way–is searching desperately for a way to save the meat sack that happens to be its vehicle in this life.

Because without the body, the brain is done, too.

What a horrible, helpless feeling that must be.

My brain isn't giving me my whole life right now, and it's certainly not giving me all my experiences. For some reason, it's only focusing on the last couple of hours. Maybe it thinks it'll find something there that'll get me out of this mess?

I don't think it'll succeed.

The long and short of it is, I realized when I was at Lucien's house that I knew more than I'd told him. Remember when I broke into that computer but didn't have a pen and paper, and just counted on my brain to remember what I was seeing? Well, it chose that moment at the table with Camille to start remembering. And it remembered some details that I hadn't even known I'd seen.

Like the addresses of the holding pens for the girls.

And the last stop in New Orleans before they boarded the ships.

I'd thought for about 2.5 seconds before deciding I had to take advantage of the new knowledge, and given it 2.5 additional seconds to go through the pros and cons of contacting Lucien and letting him know. The problem was, he was in some big meeting with people he said straight up he didn't want me meeting–the asshole–and I wasn't about to disturb him. Hell, I wasn't even sure he would answer if I called him. There was really no point in finding out.

Instead, I packed up my favorite Glock, my new butterfly knife, and my phone, and headed for the address I'd remembered as the last place the girls stopped before they were shuffled into vans and taken to the port to ship to wherever they were going.

The plan was simple: Get in, get the girls, and get back out again. The leverage: This time I had weapons and a vehicle. The danger: There were bound to be more guards than there were good guys, and I didn't have any backup.

I hadn't let that last bit stop me, though, because I wanted to get those girls out of there, and wasn't willing to wait for Lucien to get home. I found the place quickly and went in with my one gun blazing and my soul on fire with my mission, and had the good luck to find the girls almost immediately. They'd been on their own and I hadn't questioned it. I grabbed them, told them I was getting them out of there, and started running.

We made it almost all the way to the front door before the

guards found us, took one look at me, and decided I'd come back to join the party.

I put up a good fight, taking two of them out before they got my gun, but in the end I hadn't been enough—as I feared—and there were enough of them to take me down. I was handcuffed and beat up, and almost immediately found myself in the van with the other girls and on my way to the port.

Turned out I arrived just in the nick of time. If things had gone my way, I would have arrived in the nick of time, sweeping in and saving the girls right before their fates were sealed.

But things hadn't gone my way. And once again, I was in trouble and had no way to contact Lucien. And I realized–far too late–that I should have included my plan in the note I left him, instead of that clever little comment that didn't mean anything.

Once again, I'd walked right into trouble without a plan, and this time, Lucien didn't even know what I'd done. It was starting to be a really, really bad habit, and I promised myself that if I got out of this—if I managed to land on my feet again—I'd start including him in everything I did.

If.

We got to the port in the dark, the night around us quiet as a mouse, and I'd stared out the window, trying to figure out how I was going to handle this. No one was out there to save us, but they also weren't going to get in the way. If I could cause a big enough distraction, I might be able to get the girls out of there without costing myself any other lives.

An explosion would have been perfect, but I wasn't sure how to pull it off. A gunfight would have been even better, but I didn't know how the fuck I was going to pull that off without having an actual gun to hand.

Then a bunch of men appeared out of the darkness, shooting and yelling like they were actually in some sort of war, and I'd jumped to my feet. Girls were already filing off the bus ahead of me, their hands tied in front of them, and I'd gone pushing and shoving through their bodies, desperate to get outside.

Because I'd recognized one of the voices in the melee.

Lucien. Against all the odds, he'd somehow found me.

Again.

But then things went sideways and the girl I was with was caught in the crossfire. She went down and I went down over her, trying desperately to keep her from getting trampled. I realized quickly that she was going to be killed by the men around us if I didn't get her out of there, and what the fuck is the point of saving girls if you just get them killed in the end? Someone kicked me in the head and hit a spot that some other asshole had already hit me, and that had increased my motivation. I needed to get both of us out of there if we were going to live.

I made the quick decision to save myself and this girl and come back for the others—somehow—and started dragging her. We got out of the line and fire and around the corner, and there, I found a container standing open. Like it was waiting for us.

Shelter. Safety.

Maybe.

I got us inside and closed the door behind us, thinking only of stopping the bullets flying around out there, and then collapsed against the wall, my head spinning and the girl in my arms barely breathing.

And here we are.

I look down at her, taking in her too-young face and freckles, and my heart breaks. I wonder if her brain is looking for a way to survive, skipping through her memories in a desperate bid for knowledge. Trying to figure out how to heal the bullet hole in her shoulder and keep her from bleeding out. Trying to save the meat bag that is her body.

I wonder if my brain can help.

Suddenly there's a bang from the front of the container and it flies open. I cringe back, holding the girl to my chest to protect her, and glare at whoever has found his way into our shelter. My body tenses, ready to do whatever it takes to kill him. I'm unarmed and hurt, and I don't know if I can even get up, but if he comes for us my body will figure it out.

I'm fucking tired of being pushed around and beat up.

I'm itching to kill one of them, and I'm going to give my body a chance to do just that.

Then the intruder steps out of the night and into the glow of the light above him, and I gasp. That's not one of the smugglers. He's too suave, too well dressed. Far too intelligent.

And I know him. I know the man standing there like he's being lit by the sun, his eyes furious and his hand clutching a gun as his chest heaves with effort. He's both glowing and dark, the light around him disappearing into the blackness of his eyes and hair. Sharp cheekbones jut out over hollowed cheeks, and the dark bruises under his eyes tell me that he hasn't slept in days.

And God, I love him.

"Lucien," I breathe. "She's dying."

The fury melts from his face and suddenly he's on his knees next to me, his fingers on her pulse and his eyes on her face. He pauses, counting, and then looks at me. "She's still strong. I'll get someone to take her."

He makes a call on his phone, then moves the girl carefully to the side and shuffles on his knees to me. Putting a gentle hand to my forehead, he glances at what must be a bloody gash by this time, and whispers, "What happened?"

I want to make a sarcastic reply. Something funny that will push him back from me and tell him I'm okay, and that I don't need help. I want to show him I don't need anyone else and that I'm ready to go into battle, just like always.

But God, I'm so tired of pretending I can stand on my own. I haven't slept well in too long, and I've been running at full speed for as long as I can remember. I started fighting my father before I turned ten, and in New York I'm the one who always has a gun and a plan. I'm the one who always rescues my friends when they can't rescue themselves.

And fuck, I want to lean on someone else for once. I want to jump off a cliff and know someone is going to catch me. I want to fly through the air, trusting that someone will be there before I hit the ground. And Lucien is the only person I've ever known who could support me. Who *wanted* to. So for the first time in my life, I shut the sarcastic comment down and let someone in.

"A gun, I think," I whisper. "There was so much shouting and shooting, and I tried to get to the girls but the guards tried to stop me. One of them slammed a gun down on my head and I fell. But I got up, because I wasn't finished. Someone else kicked me, and then this girl got shot and I knew I had to get her to safety. And I tugged her around to–"

He stops me with a kiss, and his lips are soft and warm and wet and so comforting, and I fall into them, breathing out in relief. He's gentle with me, his hands roaming my body and looking for other wounds, and before I know it his fingertips are on my skin rather than over my clothes. They tiptoe across my belly, leaving trails of fire in their path, and my body starts to wake up.

My brain turns from the past to the present.

And the world lights up.

Lucien is everywhere. He lifts me up and leans me against the wall of the container, his tongue sliding into my mouth and his body pressing against me. He spreads his legs around mine and rises up to his full height, forcing me to tip my head back to keep kissing him. When my hands move up his stomach, seeking a resting place, he growls in deep approval and kisses me harder. The world disappears around us and it's only him and his black soul and fucking need to play hero, and I'm flying, though he's got me pinned so he can kiss me as hard as he wants.

"Woman, I'm getting really tired of finding you bruised and broken," he says, peppering kisses along the column of my neck. "And I can't believe how many times I've had to save you."

"Then stop trying to save me," I gasp, tipping my face up to the ceiling and reveling in the feel of his lips on my skin. My God, I'd forgotten how good he feels. I want his mouth on me. I want him suckling on my nipples while his fingers are busy between my legs, and then I want him to fuck me. My entire body is aching with need for him.

He jerks my chin down so I have to meet his eyes. "I will never stop trying to save you," he growls. "Not in a million years. I will always come for you, do you hear me? Always. I think it's time you accept that."

We stare at each other for a long moment, the air between us thick with the words we've never said to each other, and I realize that this is it. This is what people mean when they say they love someone so much they'd die for them.

He'd die for me.

And instead of accepting that and telling him I'd do the same for him, I've spent the last ten years running from the truth of how I feel about him.

"Lucien," I say.

He doesn't answer. He takes my shirt in his hands and rips it right down the center, exposing my body to him. And when he kisses me again, his hands are on my breasts, weighing and pinching.

This time when he breaks the kiss, his eyes are on fire. "I'm going to tie you up and keep you in my house for the rest of your life," he breathes. "I'm going to brand you as mine so that no one else ever touches you."

I thought I was already burning, but his words are like gas on an open flame, and I think this might be how I die. Heart attack from the man I've always loved telling me he's going to fucking brand me.

And because I'm not completely ready to let go of the persona I've spent ten years building, I give him the cockiest grin I can manage and tip my head. "Brand me? That's awfully gothic of you, Lucien Boudreaux."

He leans forward and takes my ear lobe in his teeth. "You have no idea what I'll do to make you mine, Brooks Landry. Try me."

His fingers go to his belt and he begins to undo it, and I'm breathless with anticipation. Yes, we're in the middle of a war and this place is overrun with enemies, but Lucien and I have been apart for too long. It feels like the universe has finally brought us back together.

And this has been building between us for a week.

Before he can pull his cock out or strip the rest of my clothes off, though, I hear a deep, sarcastic chuckle from the front of the container. It's dark and evil, and colored with a horrible sort of humor.

And I know that chuckle.

I look up, already knowing what I'm going to see, and all the fire in my veins goes ice cold.

Because my father is standing there, leaning against the door of the container like this is the most casual situation in the world. And he's smiling at me the way he used to before he hurt me.

"Christ, sweetheart, if I knew you fucked for money, I would have been able to sell you for a whole lot more."

READY FOR MORE???

Important note: Brooks' books start as companions to the Rossi series. *Dare You* happens within the confines of Rossi, as does *Tell Me*, and *Tell Me* begins Brooks and Lucien's story together. If there were things in *Pursuit* you didn't understand, they were references to *Tell Me*, which is available on all retailers.

The second half of Brooks and Lucien's story comes out in January of 2026, but I'm giving you a sneak peek of the cover, AND a not-yet-released blurb of what we're going to see next.

Lucien has saved Brooks from the human trafficking ring once, and admitted his feelings for her.

They should be in the middle of their HEA.

Instead, they've been captured by Dominick Landry and thrown into even more danger. No one knows where they are. They only have each other.

And trusting between these two sometimes-lovers-sometimes-enemies has never been more important than it is right now.

Salvation is up for preorder on all retailers, and is the second in the Brooks and Lucien duo of the New Orleans Rogues: Boudreaux series, which consists of eight books happening on one timeline.

If you haven't read the Rossi series that started it all, get into *His Romeo*, the first full-length book in Sloane and Joseph's story.

IF YOU'RE IN THE MOOD FOR SOMETHING MORE MUSICAL, TAKE A PEEK AT MY MOST BROKEN ROCK STAR YET...

Oh my God, I was kissing Noah for the second time within twenty-four hours.

Only this wasn't just kissing. It had started out that way. Noah made a joke that was obviously an attempt at being suggestive, and when I laughed, he took that as all the encouragement he needed. He'd leaned forward and brushed his lips across mine, the touch so beautiful, so gentle, that it had taken my breath away.

When I didn't pull back, he moved again, and before I knew it I was on my back on that rooftop, his arm behind my head to cushion it and his lips all over me. He kissed like he was dancing, the rhythm slow and sexy, but with a driving need that told me exactly what he had on his mind. I reached up and wrapped my fingers in his hair, savoring the feel of him there. I couldn't believe this was happening.

Again.

The world spun around me and I wondered for a moment if I was getting drunk off the alcohol on his breath. Or was it soaking out of his skin and right into mine?

Wait, maybe I was just drunk. I'd been drinking, too, so that must be it. Why else would I be taking this chance? We were on the fucking roof, for God's sake, the sky open and painted in technicolor above us as the sunset washed over the sky. He moved to settle between my legs and I opened for him, my heart hammering with how much I wanted him. Fucking hell, I was aching in places I didn't even know you could ache and I felt like my heart was going to explode. He pushed against me then, his cock hard and ready, and I moaned up into his mouth.

He broke the kiss almost as quickly as he'd started it. "Fuck, Molly," he gasped, rocking his hips again and again. "Fuck, I want you."

"Want me?" I asked. "You've barely even started kissing me."

He dove back to his work, and now the hand that wasn't cradling my head went to work. He slid my t-shirt up far enough to expose the skin of my stomach and let his fingertips slide along the top of my pajama bottoms. And God help me, I nearly bucked with how good it felt. Butterflies exploded through my veins and into my stomach, flying quickly to the space between my legs, where I was now burning. I used my grip on his head to pull him deeper into the kiss, our tongues dancing together as if we'd done this a million times.

It felt like we had. My body knew his like it had already had him, both of us moving in tandem as we rocked together. His cock pushed harder against me and I squirmed, wanting more, but his body pressed down on me, holding me still.

"Christ, girl, stop moving like that," he moaned. "You're going to make me lose control."

I giggled at that. I couldn't help myself. "Control? You just jumped me on the rooftop of the hotel where we're staying.

Anyone could walk out here and see us. That wouldn't be good for you, and it wouldn't be good for me. And you're talking about control?"

He leaned down and dragged his teeth along the skin beneath my ear. "Does that mean you want to stop?"

His fingers dipped lower, slipping under the waistband of my pajamas, and then into my panties. Every inch of me stilled with anticipation of his touch going lower, and I forgot how to breathe.

"No," I breathed. "Don't stop."

"Aw, you want me to keep going?" he teased. "And here I thought you were mad at me."

I was, I recalled. There was something wrong, here. I could remember that much. I wasn't supposed to be doing this, and I sure as hell wasn't supposed to be enjoying it as much as I was. But I couldn't remember why. All I knew was he smelled like cigarettes and alcohol and the world around us was filled with magic. The sky was pink and purple and he was so fucking warm.

So close.

So hard.

"Please," I said. I didn't know what I was asking for. I just knew I needed it.

He pulled back and stared down at me, his eyes darker than I'd ever seen them. "Please what?"

And fuck, it was all too much. He was so beautiful, so familiar. This was everything I'd ever wanted from him, and I'd never seen it before. But now that we were here...

I didn't want it to happen on the roof, with a rock digging into my back. I didn't want to rush through in the fear that someone would come out and see us.

I wanted him all to myself. For once in my life.

"Take me to your room," I said.

The grin that blossomed over his face was so beautiful, so

mischievous, that if I hadn't already been in love with him, I would have promptly fallen. He stood up and bent to scoop me into his arms, his nose buried in my neck as if he couldn't stop himself.

"You're so beautiful," he breathed. "Which room are you in?"

"Why are we going to mine?" I asked, surprised. I'd asked for his.

"Because no one will look for us there. And I want to take my time with you."

That sounded pretty much perfect to me. And though I'd tried to remember why this was a bad idea, I let it slip into the air around us. I didn't want to stop. I wanted to let him have his way with me. I was in a strange town, with a new job, and we were on tour. No one would ever know.

Right?

"Stop thinking," he rumbled. "And tell me where your room is."

Noah made love to me the same way he'd kissed me. He stripped me slowly, taking his time and kissing every inch of my skin as he went. When I was laying in nothing but bra and panties he reared back and stared at me for so long I started squirming.

"Did you undress me just to stare at me?" I asked.

He leaned down and pressed a kiss between my breasts. "I'm admiring you," he said quietly when he looked up again. His blue eyes were trouble, now, and I realized he knew exactly what he was doing. "You're fucking gorgeous, and I've never slowed down long enough to appreciate it."

I could have said that was his own fault, or given him trouble for not paying attention. But his fingers were moving down my belly and into my panties, and I'd stopped caring. He stripped my panties down my legs, then deftly unhooked my bra, and a moment later he was between my legs again, the head of his cock nudging at my opening.

"Is this okay?" he asked.

Oh my God, he was going to kill me. "Stop asking stupid questions. Do you think I'd be here if it wasn't?"

His mouth curled in a slow smile. "You never do things you don't want to do."

That wasn't strictly true. But I wasn't going to waste time arguing with him about it. Besides, he was already starting to push into me. And he was so big, so hard, that smile still curving his lush lips, that I was going to lose my mind. I stopped breathing and tilted my hips to take him, his cock stretching me and filling me up until I thought I would explode.

And fuck, when he started to move, I knew I would.

He was slow and tender, taking my hands in his and stretching them out to the side so I was spread open for him as he took me. He never stopped staring, pinning my gaze with his own as he moved in and out, in and out, going so slow that I wanted to scream.

Or tell him to never stop. I wasn't sure which.

When the pressure started to build inside me, though, I wrapped my legs around his waist and pulled him closer. "Stop being so gentle," I told him.

He closed his eyes, the strain on his face unreal. "You're so small. I don't want to hurt you."

I yanked hand out of his grip and put it to his face, suddenly impatient. "You're not going to. And I'm tired of being treated like I might break."

He opened his eyes and stared at me for a second.

And then he started moving faster, pounding into me harder. In and out and then back in again as my body took every blow, rising up to meet him and take him deeper. And fuck, this was everything. All of my focus narrowed down on that point of contact between us, where he was reaching deeper and deeper into me, building something that I couldn't hold inside. My body was getting more coiled with every thrust, an earthquake building inside me, and when he finally released my eyes and bent down over me, taking my ear in his teeth and groaning deeply with need, I knew I wasn't going to be able to hold onto it much longer.

He was driving me right to the edge, and I wanted to take him with me.

"Noah," I gasped. "Please. God, please."

"Please what, Bug?"

His voice was husky and strained, but it was the nickname that drove me into the light. He'd called me that from the first day we met, and it had always meant safety. Security. Someone at my back.

It had always meant Noah.

I exploded for him them, crying out in abandon, and he flew into the orgasm with me, pumping into me as my body opened up even further for him, his face buried in my neck and my name on his lips.

Noah is now available on all retailers!

SOUNDTRACK

When it came to writing *Pursuit*, I didn't use a soundtrack. I had a few songs on constant repeat.

Supermodel, Maneskin
    Gossip, Maneskin feat the unreal Tom Morello (patriot and rockstar)
    Wild Child, The Black Keys (this is Brooks' song)
    Money Maker, The Black Keys
    Hell of a Season, The Black Keys
    Lonely Boy, The Black Keys
    Unstoppable, The Score
    Only One, The Score
    Shakedown, The Score

ABOUT THE AUTHOR

Bestselling author Quinn Marlowe is a fan of red wine, cheesecake, perfect hash browns, and really good punk rock. She's also obsessed with everything piratical—though she refuses to acknowledge any actual connection to pirates. She studied English and Film at UCLA and, when forced to choose a career, chose publishing rather than teaching or being a film maker.

Quinn is now happily playing the villain in a certain man's story, and loving every minute of her freedom. She lives in San Diego with her dogs, the ducks that moved into the front yard, and far too many cats.

ALSO BY QUINN MARLOWE

NEW YORK ROGUES: ROSSI, THE ANNIVERSARY COLLECTION

His Obsession

Her Romeo

Her Hero

Her Target

Her Keeper

Her Rebellion

Her Master

And some duos. Special formatting. Sneak peeks. All-new covers.

New York Rogues: Rossi, The Anniversary Collection, the Sloane and Joseph Edit

New York Rogues: Rossi, The Anniversary Collection, the Michael and Penny Edit

New York Rogues: Rossi, The Anniversary Collection, the Dax and Dante Edit

NEW YORK ROGUES: BROOKS PETERSON

Dare You

Tell Me

NEW ORLEANS ROGUES: BOUDREAUX

Pursuit

Salvation, now available for preorder

Escape, now available for preorder

ROCK & ROLL NIGHTS

Rivers: Tattoos and Heartbreak

Rivers: Guitars and Mistakes

Rock & Roll Nights

Noah: Smoke and Mirrors

SOUTHERN HEROES

Christmas Music

Hero in Waiting

Hero Next Door

Hero on the Road

If you're in the mood for something darker...

The Hawke's Bounty series. MFM. Age gap. Poly. Forced proximity. Bounty hunters and the romance that blooms between kidnappers and their captives.

Start with *Taken*, coming this fall

The Hawke's Wood series. MFM. Age gap. Stepdad/stepbrother. Forced proximity. Small town. Snowed in. A cast of small town men and the girls who come to stay.

Start with *Little Bird,* coming this fall

For more details—and sneak peeks—follow me at Substack.